Double the
Stars

KELLEY SWAIN

Published by Cinnamon Press,
Meirion House,
Tanygrisiau,
Blaenau Ffestiniog,
Gwynedd LL41 3SU
www.cinnamonpress.com

ISBN 978-1-909077-36-2

British Library Cataloguing in Publication Data. A CIP record for this book can be obtained from the British Library.

Designed and typeset in Garamond by Cinnamon Press. Cover design by Cassie Herschel-Shorland and Jan Fortune from custom hand-made paper-cut artwork 'Caroline Herschel' by Cassie Herschel-Shorland © used by kind permission.

Cinnamon Press is represented by Inpress and by the Welsh Books Council in Wales.

Printed in Poland

To my mother, Kathleen Swain,
for being a woman of science.
And for love and support, always.

And

To Cassie Herschel-Shorland,
and her father John Herschel-Shorland
for generosity, inspiration, and friendship.

Double the Stars

Chapter 1

1782

Caroline's introduction to England came in a series of jolts. First, the ship carrying her and her brother William across the Channel ran aground. Next, the sailor helping sea-swamped passengers ashore deposited her on the rocky coast of Dover like a sack of coal. Then, the small, contained world of their carriage to London turned to chaos when one of the horses took fright and bolted, overturning the whole vehicle. When they finally arrived in Bath, Caroline slept for three days.

Back then, her English was so poor she relied upon William to translate the passengers' shouts and curses. Back then, her hands were chapped and raw from the chores their mother demanded. Back then, her hair was tangled and her cheeks reddened from their wagon ride across the wind-blasted dykes of Holland. On the journey, her linen cap had blown away.

Now, impeccably groomed, Caroline stood before William in the siblings' comfortable home in New King Street. There, she and her two brothers had established themselves in a trio of musical skills: composition, teaching, performance. Only last season, she had sung as first soprano in William's choir at the Octagon Chapel. But life, like a ship, could appear on an even keel one moment, and lurch upon unseen rocks the next.

'Carolina, Alexander, I have marvellous news,' William announced, waving a letter which drooped with the heaviest of seals. 'His Royal Highness, delighted by my discovery, summons me to Windsor. He wishes for me to personally show him the planet which bears his name.'

'Well done, naming it the *Georgium Sidus*,' Alexander said. 'The first planet to be discovered since the Ancients mapped the Heavens – what King would not be pleased?'

Caroline winced. William fancied taking after Galileo, who'd named the moons of Jupiter the Medician Stars, seeking support from those Royal brothers. The act was a downright request for patronage.

'I…hadn't fancied it would *work*,' she murmured. Her weak eye fluttered and she waved her hand across her face to hide it, a habit she thought she'd broken once she'd begun to perform.

'My bid to catch the King?' William said, his ears sharp as his eyesight. He leaned back in his chair and crossed his arms, appraising the letter on the desk. A smile spread across his face. 'But it *has* worked, Sister. Have you anything else to say?'

Caroline gripped the back of the slipper chair where her brothers took turns practising the cello, violin, and guitar. Her elbow bumped the cello and it fell to the carpet with a resonant groan. Alexander gave a start, but William only watched with a level gaze.

'Forgive me,' she said, straightening the instrument. 'It's unharmed.'

'I know, Lina, it has suffered worse knocks,' William said, his brown eyes lively. She knew how pleased he was to receive the letter, but she'd be hanged if she let him turn this into a celebration. She frowned.

'I am going to Windsor, Sister, and God willing, I shall be given a place there, to carry out my research. You will, of course, join me. Have you no thoughts on the matter?' He spoke gently, but there was no room for negotiation.

Alexander chuckled. 'God willing? Nay, *His Majesty* willing.'

'I have thoughts, William,' she said, ignoring their younger brother. 'Frankly, I am overwhelmed with them.'

I wish you a safe journey, and of course, I wish you success. How can I not? I wish you success with all of your endeavours. But to say I would be pleased to quit Bath, to end our musical careers here? That I cannot do.'

'Fairly spoken,' William said, as Alexander nodded. 'But consider this while I'm away: we may not remain long in Bath. My absence may provide time to adapt to the idea. I hope so, Sister.' He rose. 'Lend a hand, Alex. We'll pack the scopes with care. They must work perfectly for His Majesty.'

When, Caroline wondered, had this hobby taken over their lives? She made her way to the attic room she shared with Alexander, arms full of rumpled lace. Shirt cuffs her brothers ruined again and again, caught on a lathe or splashed with pitch. All for making telescopes. She shook her head. They never tore or stained their cuffs when working at music.

What would their father think if he still lived? Isaac had worked his way from an inherited position as gardener, into the prestigious Band of the Hanoverian Guards, and had shared his love for music with all of his children. Even Caroline enjoyed brief tutorials, but only when Frau Herschel was not at home. Frau Herschel had never wanted her youngest daughter to learn skills that might encourage independence. Caroline stabbed the needle fiercely through the fabric. A less dextrous seamstress might have drawn blood. Only her hard-won skills at stitching could restore the cuffs to respectability.

Their father, not wishing to be a gardener, had sought a tutor in music. Cleverness and good manners were his guides. Caroline, near the age young Isaac had been when he first tucked a violin beneath his chin, had sat by the sewing-table of one Miss Carsten. This sweet unfortunate lady was known for two things: she was the deftest needle-worker in Hanover and she was doomed to die young. Poor Miss Carsten suffered consumption, and her fine lace kerchiefs were embroidered, quite secretly, with specks of blood.

Back then, Caroline had wondered whether it would be better to be beautiful, though ill, like Miss Carsten, or sturdy, yet ugly, like herself. Caroline had been struck with Typhus as a child, the same fever which carried one of her younger siblings to the grave. The fever, and a bout of smallpox shortly after, had left her with a weak, squinting eye, marked skin, and a crabbed physique. The only positive result, other than, she supposed, not dying, was that she seemed impenetrable henceforth to illness.

'Sister!' Alexander's shout up the stairs broke Caroline's thoughts. 'We've packed the scopes and readied the horses; wrap us some food for the journey?'

Caroline folded the cuff and set it aside: a small start to the mountain on the bed.

Outside the house, the driver of the cart carrying the telescopes awaited William's instructions. If the weather held, the travellers would reach Windsor Castle by next midday. The light waned ever shorter as autumn pressed on, and William could cover ground more quickly by himself, but he would stay with the scopes. They were worth a King's ransom – or patronage, which amounted to the same thing.

The brothers made each beautiful object entirely by hand. Alex spent hours crafting the wooden bodies on his lathe, trailing sweet-smelling sawdust that Caroline constantly brushed from the furniture and beat from the rugs. The hearth never wanted kindling, with all the pieces Alexander cast off in turning mounts and bodies for their scopes. Sometimes Caroline considered the raw blocks of wood from which her brother carved such smooth shapes, and wondered if the telescope was somehow already inside, awaiting release. Trees' branches aspired toward the sun; could not their cores stretch for the stars?

In his workshop adjoining the kitchen, William would disappear for days at a time, smelting, grinding, and polishing the telescopes' metal mirrors. He'd devised charts and graphs for how many strokes of the polishing steel had to go left-to-right, up-to-down, clockwise or anti. This method gave his lenses the greatest magnification of any reflecting telescope to date, but if he was interrupted in a pattern of polishing, a speculum could be ruined. The process also ruined his clothes, and cloying smells crept under the workshop door into her kitchen. When William made specula, Caroline did her best to combat the stench of pitch and iron with fragrant rosemary and bay.

Sometimes her brothers asked her to varnish the wood of the scopes, but her main job was to write, in tidy script, the detailed instruction manuals for assembling and operating the instruments. They were shipped all over the world, to men who paid handsomely for the best telescopes available, better even than those used by the Astronomer Royal.

'Here we are, Brother, a chicken and ham pie, and this lovely cheese,' Caroline said, handing William a cloth-wrapped parcel tied with twine. 'More than enough until tomorrow, when you shall be feasting with His Highness, no doubt,' she added, raising an eyebrow.

William returned the look before packing the bundle into his saddlebag. 'That's my hope, Sister. And I'll write immediately upon discovering the King's plans for my skills.'

'Mind your words, Brother,' Alexander said, 'or Caroline will debate that your skills are best used conducting at the Octagon, or composing, or teaching music – anything to remain in Bath.'

William chuckled, and Caroline bit her lip, for those thoughts had been perched on her tongue. How could they treat this possible revolution with such levity? It was as if she were Copernicus, announcing the sun was in fact the centre of the universe, and everyone was jeering. Or perhaps William had the part of Copernicus, announcing this revision of their world. But no: music was their centre. It always had been.

'Well then, I am away,' William said, securing the final buckle on his pack. Alexander stepped forward to shake his brother's hand. 'Our thoughts will travel with you. You have the finest references and scopes – I needn't wish you luck.'

'Lina,' William moved to embrace Caroline. She hugged him close. He smelled of tar, vanilla, and home. She wished she could reach into his head and understand the thoughts within.

'I agree, you don't need luck, but I shall wish it for you nonetheless,' she said quietly, hoping both that he would succeed, and, somehow, change his mind. She could never wish him failure.

He kissed her forehead and smiled. 'Then I shall have luck, whether I need it or not,' he said. 'Safe against uncertainty.'

He gestured to the driver of the cart to be off before mounting his grey mare, flipping back his coattails as he settled into the saddle. The young horse let out a snuffle, eager for the journey. Waving, William nudged the mare down the road, and the white stone houses and glinting windows of New King Street seemed to watch him go.

Chapter 2

William's departure for Windsor renewed an old pain in Caroline. When they were young, whenever he had left, it signalled life-changing upheaval. Not for her, though: never for her. She had been always stuck at home, a drudge to their mother's incessant demands: cooking, washing, scrubbing, laundry.

When Caroline was ten years old, William joined Father in the Hanoverian Guards. But war broke out, and William disappeared. Though he was too young to be officially condemned as a deserter, the family remained secretive, wary for his safety. No one would tell Caroline what had happened to her favourite brother. One night, she saw William whispering in the courtyard with their mother. Frau Herschel refused to utter a word about it, though Caroline clutched at her mother's skirts and begged. Much later, she learned William had fled to England.

Whenever she could escape Frau Herschel's notice, Caroline pored over the books he'd left behind. They spoke of the haste of his flight, for they were expensive, and he surely wanted them. *Leibnitz, Newton, Euler… Sidereus Nuncius*. She ran her small finger along the gilded letters.

'It's called *The Starry Messenger,* Alex, listen,' William's voice, not yet broken to the timbre of manhood, sounded in her mind. *She* used to listen, through the wall, to William's chatter, long after she knew Alexander had fallen asleep.

'Galileo looked through this homemade contraption called a telescope and viewed hundreds more stars than we can see with our eyes alone…' His awe rang in Caroline's ears even now.

Perhaps those books had seeded this interest in astronomy, she thought, scrubbing the honey-coloured Bath flagstones in the kitchen. She had never before connected those young ramblings with stargazing, but William's books had certainly urged him to turn his attention to the sky.

On the day after William left for his audience with the King, Alexander departed for London to perform in a concert, leaving Caroline to a quiet house. She rose early, and it took her the day to beat rugs, scrub floors, and wash windows. With no pairs of boots tramping sand, sawdust and dirt across the carpets, Caroline felt bereft. There was no one to feed but herself, and the mountain of ruined cuffs disappeared, replaced with a pile of repaired lace. It only took half the following day to polish the silver, wax the furniture, and tune the instruments. She wrung her hands at the thought that the cosy terraced house was tidier than it had been since they moved in, and they might soon leave it behind.

This feeling in her stomach of quietly aching pleasure and regret, as if she'd drunk sweetened milk that was on the verge of going sour, was not new. It was a brew of excitement, uncertainty, and anticipation. The time around her twenty-first birthday had been a similar mix of sweet and sour.

Miss Carsten succumbed to her consumption only weeks before Caroline's birthday. Caroline swallowed this sadness to care for her father, who had developed a troubling cough of his own. During the war, he had lain in flooded trenches, and the damp had crept into his bones, leaving him feeling forever warped and out of tune. Without the energy to sing or play, Isaac sat by the fire copying musical scores. Though Caroline was nurse to her ailing father, the quiet presence in the room, of the other person, was the balm each needed. Though

14

Isaac was ill, he assured his daughter that her company helped him to feel as well as he could.

Frau Herschel, unwilling or unable to bear the sight of her sickly husband, was often away, clucking amongst the other matrons of the village. Jacob, the eldest, was rarely home. Father never failed to ask him if he had sold any music, but Jacob would announce that he had yet to find a buyer who would pay the asking price. Father suggested that the asking price might be too high, even for a musician of the Hanoverian Court, but Jacob waved the advice away. He dressed in what Caroline supposed were the latest fashions, came home late, smelling of wine, and bossed Caroline about as if she were a common servant. After Frau Herschel, Jacob was the second person she most wished to avoid.

Shortly after Caroline learned of Miss Carsten's death, Isaac died, leaving Jacob as head of the house. The flavour of sourness became constant. Caroline would enter the room where her father usually sat correcting scores, and the lack of him in his chair would hit her in the stomach, taking her breath away.

Grief was a constellation of dirty soap bubbles, for Frau Herschel mourned by putting Caroline to work. She was used to the labour, but now she felt alone in the world. William and Alexander were building musical careers in England, and only William and Isaac had paid her any heed, or showed her any affection. With no kind words to look forward to, and no prospect, under her mother's narrow gaze, of becoming a seamstress or governess, Caroline despaired.

So grim were these months, the unexpected arrival of a letter from William was the sweetest draught Caroline had ever tasted. Her stagnant life effervesced with unhoped-for possibility. After reading the letter, she wept into her blankets at the top of the apartment in Hanover.

The letter announced William's plan to bring Caroline to Bath. He and Alexander wanted Frau Herschel to relinquish her daughter so the brothers might have an assistant and housekeeper in their bachelor home, and Caroline might have the opportunity to train as a singer. William knew Caroline had a promising voice, and there might be a chance, he wrote, for her to perform.

Caroline read all of this to Frau Herschel, as she had done since she was a small girl, reading the post aloud, and writing correspondence as it was dictated. She spoke slowly, controlling the trembling in her voice. Secretly, she feared the prospect of singing, for she had not sung in years, but the whisper of freedom fixed her resolve to go.

'Nein.'

Frau Herschel flattened William's proposal with a single, curt word. She plucked the letter from Caroline's hands and it disappeared into a pocket in her skirts.

It didn't matter – Caroline had already memorised every line.

This time, she did not allow grief to consume her. She threw herself into daily tasks, giving her mother no cause for complaint. At night, she knitted stocking after stocking for Jacob so he would not be left wanting when William came to take her away. She learned to subsist on little sleep. She tied a gag of cloth around her mouth and practised singing, as she had heard was done by ladies of the opera. And she dreamt of England.

On the day he came to collect her, William's voice sparred with Frau Herschel's shouts through the thick oak door. Caroline paced the hall, wringing her hands until they burned. The fact was, it was Jacob's decision to relinquish any hold on Caroline, and he was away performing in the Court Band. He wouldn't care whether she lived or died, not least whether she remained or stayed. Frau Herschel knew this, yet the miserly woman wasn't pleased at the prospect of losing her unpaid servant.

Reckless, Caroline pressed her ear to the door.

'I know Lina did not have as many opportunities to learn music as we did, but she could do so in England,' William said. He did not add that those lost chances were due to Frau Herschel.

A rustle, and a sniff. 'I simply don't know what I'd do without her.'

There was a pause, and Caroline's weak eye began to flutter. Was that it? Would her favourite brother give up on her?

'Wait,' William said. Caroline pressed her ear harder to the door. 'I will provide for you,' his voice dropped to a growl, 'the cost of keeping one servant. As I understand Carolina's…*indispensability*…to you.'

Caroline feared her pounding heart would cause the door to rattle.

'You really *should* ask Jacob,' Frau Herschel said.

The journey to the coast was a mixture of terror and exhilaration. For six days and nights, Caroline clung to the thin railing on top of the Post-waggon, grateful for William's solid warmth beside her.

They ate apples and tossed the cores into the dusty road, watching the browned stubs disappear as the carriage rolled across Holland. They took it in turns to nap on each other's shoulder. Through the cool, dewy nights, they worked together to tuck the edges of their only woollen blanket around them, huddling like a pair of doves in a hayloft. They counted windmills and bridges, William making Caroline repeat the English words. The sky burned brilliant with stars, more than Caroline had ever seen peeking between the crooked rooftops of

Hanover. William began to teach her, in English, the summer zodiac and other simple constellations.

From the tidy, empty house in New King Street, Caroline wondered if William's journey to collect her was the true starting point for his obsession with the sky. On that ride across Holland, there seemed enough stars for both of them to be lost in forever.

Chapter 3

'Thank you,' Caroline said to the postman, tying the strings of her purse. Usually she fretted over the expense of every letter delivered, but this was from William. She latched the door and hastened to the standing desk her brothers had built.

'To protect your voice, Lina. You mustn't be hunched in a chair half the day,' William had said. She'd grown used to standing for hours on end, copying his orchestral scores, or re-writing, in a fair hand, his scientific papers for the newly formed Royal Society, the members of which seemed only to encourage his strange hobby.

She broke open the letter and hurriedly took in William's scrawl. Her shoulders dropped. He still waited to meet the King. Nothing official, then: not yet. However, William had been invited to demonstrate his telescopes to some of the Court, and the Princesses had requested a viewing. The evening, to William's dismay, had been cloudy. Ever resourceful, he set up a pasteboard cut-out of Saturn, to be spied down the hill from the telescope on the castle parapet. The Princesses had been delighted.

'The effect was so natural,' he wrote, 'that even the best astronomer might have been deceived.'

Caroline could not help but smile at his resourcefulness. The long-case clock ticked comfortingly as she read through his letter several times. He had met with Dr Maskelyne, the Astronomer Royal, who had confirmed that the Herschel's telescopes were superior to any at the Royal Observatory in Greenwich, and had placed an order with William for a new reflector. Caroline felt her cheeks growing warm, recalling their first encounter with that striking, white-haired man.

*

William had been far back in the garden behind the house, nearly where the lawn met the river, viewing the clear summer skies from his seven-foot telescope. Caroline was gathering her writing materials and preparing to join her brother when the doorbell chimed.

Though once an oddity to have guests so late, as word of William's homemade telescopes spread, their number of night-time visitors increased. Caroline opened the door to greet their young friend, Dr William Watson, and a gentleman whom she didn't recognise.

'Good evening, Miss Herschel,' Dr Watson said, making a little bow. 'I noticed the candle burning at the window,' he gestured towards the parlour, 'and took the risk of calling. Is your brother about?'

Caroline showed the men downstairs before retreating to the kitchen, where she set about stoking the hearth. She slid the coffee-box from the hiding-stone in the wall and unlocked it. The later the hour, the colder the night, the more welcome a hot dish of coffee. By the time she made her way into the garden with a tray, the stranger and William were conversing in pitched tones.

'Oh dear,' she whispered to Dr Watson, 'I hope my brother hasn't caused offence.'

Watson shook his head, murmuring his thanks for the coffee. 'Certainly not, Miss Herschel. It's only natural for sparks to fly between two such inquisitive minds.' Caroline nodded and excused herself to offer coffee to the others.

'And how do you fare, Miss Herschel, as assistant to such an inventor as your brother?' the stranger asked, drawing a smile from William. Introductions had been forgotten, but Caroline felt too shy to draw attention to the error.

'It certainly is a challenge, Sir, adjusting to this hobby of William's,' she admitted, 'but he ensures I learn all I need to in order to adequately help.'

William nodded his encouragement, his eyes squinting in pleasure as he took a long drink.

'What are you working on at present?' asked the visitor.

'At the moment, I'm calculating the minutes of arc of double stars which William finds in his sweeps, and comparing certain nebulous clusters with Messier's notations – you know of Messier, the French astronomer, Sir?'

The man chuckled. 'I do, Miss Herschel. That is impressive work for a young lady.'

'No one takes such precise notes, nor carries out such accurate calculations, as my sister,' William affirmed.

'I'm just…minding the heavens, really,' Caroline stammered, surprised she had spoken at such length. She gathered the tray and hastened indoors.

William entered the kitchen in high spirits after the gentlemen took their leave. 'There's a devil of a fellow!' he cried. 'And he expressly said that he valued your input.'

'Oh, no, I'm sure I spoke too freely,' Caroline said. 'Who was he? I wasn't introduced.'

'Who *was* he?' William repeated, breaking into a peal of laughter. 'Why, Nevil Maskelyne, my dear. None other than the Astronomer Royal.'

And now, Caroline thought, her eyes scanning each tangled loop and line from William's pen, Dr Maskelyne had travelled to Windsor, to champion her brother's cause.

The Maskelynes – both Nevil and his wife, Sophia – had been supporters of William's work since that night the men first met. Letters describing ideas, discoveries, and advice travelled back and forth between the Royal Observatory and New King Street. They'd invited Caroline to Greenwich a score of times, but she had yet to make the journey.

Despite her wish for their lives to remain focused on music, Caroline hoped, for her brother's sake, that Dr Maskelyne's support would encourage the King's favour. The thought of William's disappointment was far more troubling than her own uncertainty.

Chapter 4

The following afternoon, Caroline entered the New Assembly Rooms as quietly as she could, but people turned to look nonetheless. The *bon ton* monitored the comings and goings of everyone, however unimportant. And, as William Herschel's sister, and first soprano at the Octagon, Caroline was not unimportant. The lady she was meeting spotted her and swept over, appearing to revel in the very ostentation Caroline preferred to avoid.

'My dear Miss Herschel, *such* a delight to see you,' Mrs Colebrook trilled over the tunes of an orchestra.

The widow Colebrook took great pleasure in assessing Caroline's appearance each time they met. As she unwrapped her woollen shawl, Caroline hoped her friend would approve of the low-necked dress of bluebell-coloured silk, which draped to the floor with a full, sweeping skirt. A froth of lace, tucked in at the bodice, modestly covered her décolletage, shoulders, and neck, and matched the belled lace of her cuffs, spilling from the mid-length sleeves of the dress. It was the latest fashion, which Caroline had discovered from the ladies of the Octagon choir. Though she rarely bought new fabric – hating to spend a penny more than necessary – she was adept at altering her old dresses. She was grateful that styles appeared to be tending towards practicality and simplicity since her move to England. Upon arrival in the country, fashions had been French, and enormous. Caroline could hardly walk in the pannier-laden skirts; she could barely breathe in her boned stays.

For this meeting, she had piled and pinned her thick curls high on her head, leaving a few ringlets spilling down. And, with an expert touch borne of practise, she always made use of a powder Mrs Colebrook gave her. It was an annual Christmas gift, begun on their trip to London years ago. The powder was magic, smoothing her pocked skin to the creamy porcelain of an English rose. The faintest touches of rouge on the cheeks and a tint to the lips, also the lessons of Mrs Colebrook, finished the look, so Caroline could stand in the candlelit rooms of the Octagon and cause neither a positive nor negative sensation. She would never be pretty, but she could be pleasant.

This did not stop the fluttering in her stomach when she stepped into the gilded brightness of the New Assembly Rooms. Though she was fit to be seen, Caroline was never certain she would grow accustomed to it. As a child, she had been ignored by everyone but Father and William. And it was always a shock to meet someone's gaze. She was also uncomfortably aware that her petite stature made her appear twenty-two rather than thirty-two years of age.

'You look very sweet indeed, my dear girl,' Mrs Colebrook declared as Caroline curtsied in front of her. 'But perhaps we'll fit you out with a hat later on.'

Caroline turned a grimace into a smile and followed the lady towards the pillared Tea Room, where the orchestra played from a high gallery. William had asked Mrs Colebrook to take Caroline under her wing when he'd first brought his sister to Bath. Caroline needed to learn English dress, customs, and habits, as well as the language. Mrs Colebrook took her on as a pet project, which Caroline had been grateful for at the time.

Though she didn't know much English when they first met, it hadn't taken her long to realise Mrs Colebrook's real reasons for adopting her with such enthusiasm. The rich widow was near to William's age, and young enough to be expected to remarry. She was his most eager student, paying him well to ride out to her country estate for private lessons at the pianoforte, or guitar, when that instrument was briefly fashionable. She was a regular presence at the Octagon, and encouraged other people of good standing to attend.

With fiery red hair and handsome features, Cecelia Colebrook undoubtedly *would* remarry – but Caroline knew it would not be to William. Mrs Colebrook did not see it, but William treated the widow just the same as his other students. He rode out to Bath Easton with no greater enthusiasm than he rode out to other country homes. In short, he appeared unaware of Mrs Colebrook's affections.

At first, this had only encouraged the lady to try harder. She had invited both William and Caroline to play whist with herself, the Marchioness of Denby, and Mr Palmer, one of the patrons of the Octagon. And in a grand gesture, she had taken Caroline off to London for six full weeks during the winter season.

Caroline had been nearly twenty-four. Perhaps the widow had been hoping she'd meet a beau and marry, leaving William wanting a woman's presence in the home. In London they attended everything from the Opera and dances at the Pantheon to auctions and Masquerades. Caroline was subjected to hairdressers, lace shawls, carriages and ball gowns. She'd listened carefully to phrases and pronunciation, and had tried her best to imitate mannerisms – the flick of a fan, the sweep of a skirt. Mrs Colebrook chided her for frowning with concentration.

'A young lady,' the widow said, 'should always smile with pleasure in such grand settings.'

The hubbub of evening galas became a blur.

'Look there, Miss Herschel – the Duchess of Devonshire! Pray, pay attention to *her* dress, for it will always be taken up as the newest fashion.'

Caroline declined invitations to dance, for she did not know the steps. Inside, she burned with shame. If only Frau Herschel had not barred her from dancing lessons so long ago; but dancing was one of the many skills Caroline had failed to learn in her efforts to become a governess. She was horrified to vex Mrs Colebrook, who sat beside her charge while the company twirled merrily before them.

'We shall hire a dancing mistress for you upon your return to Bath, my dear,' Mrs Colebrook had said, patting Caroline's hand. 'Then you may say yes to these charming suitors.'

The offers to dance had baffled Caroline. She supposed it must be to do with the powder, the rouge, the dress. No matter how cheerful they seemed, the thought of dancing with young men whom she didn't know had frightened her more than the foreignness of the dances.

They bought tea at Twinings on the Strand, toured the Wedgwood showroom, and purchased haberdashery at Grafton House. Caroline bought Italian Parmesan for William at the Haymarket. At the auction rooms Mrs Colebrook bid on a pair of carriage horses, simply because Caroline declared them a pretty pair of steeds. The ladies later discovered, to Caroline's horror and Mrs Colebrook's amusement, that the horses were both blind.

Only days before they planned to return to Bath, a snowstorm hit, closing the roads and trapping Caroline with her chaperone for two further weeks. The widow was not unkind, but Caroline felt she might go mad with her friend's nonsensical chatter. Caroline ached to return to Bath. She missed William's 'Lessons for Lina,' which echoed those hasty tutorials from Father that Frau Herschel forbade. William would work straight through breakfast to teach her English, arithmetic, and music. She missed the long garden and messy workshop behind the house at New King Street. She missed Alexander's violin solos and William's oboe concertos. Never, since Hanover, had she been more ready to assist William at whatever he needed, whether polishing lenses or copying scores.

When the roads finally reopened, the ladies embarked upon their journey home. The maid fainted in the confines of the carriage; Caroline opened the windows and fanned the girl to revive her. Mrs Colebrook flew into hysterics over the 'shocking episode'; Caroline passed around smelling salts. After an interminably chilly, jolting drive, sloshing through mud and melting snow, Caroline heaved an unladylike sigh of relief upon glimpsing the sand-coloured terraces and cobbled streets of Bath.

Mrs Colebrook's manners towards Caroline in the New Assembly Rooms did not have quite the same warmth as on that trip to London. They settled at a small table, were served afternoon tea, and Mrs Colebrook launched into her usual gossip about people in whom Caroline had no interest. Biting into a scone, Caroline bit back the desire to scandalise her friend by announcing William's plan to give up music. But she only sipped her tea and pretended to listen. She herself was shocked by the prospect, and until it was confirmed, she did not wish to announce it.

How horrified the widow had been when confronted with William's hobby – yet, it was far from secret. The music room had maps strewn across the angled top of the spinet, pasteboard telescope tubes piled in the corner beside the cello, and an astrolabe propped against the metronome. For each musical instrument, there was an astronomical equivalent; a layperson mightn't be able to distinguish which device was for which purpose. Students forgave William his eccentricity, as he was a gentleman and skilled tutor. They indulged his philosophical ramblings when his lectures veered from harmonics of music to harmonies of the celestial spheres. But William had tried Mrs Colebrook's patience too far during one of her lessons in town.

Caroline had been making her way to the attic with a pile of mending when she and her friend nearly collided on the stairs.

'What's the trouble, dear?' Caroline asked, trying not to dwell on the waste of time that would surely result from the question.

'That man!' Mrs Colebrook spat. Her cheeks were red as her hair. 'I do not know why he pretends to teach music, with his head so far in the clouds. He hardly paid me any attention, and only set me practising whilst busying himself with charts and numbers.' She paused to catch her breath before flaring again. 'Good day, Miss Herschel – do inform you brother that I shall be pleased to resume as his *student* when he resumes an interest in *teaching*.' At that, she swept down the stairs and out the door.

Baffled, Caroline dropped the clothing on her bed before hurrying to peek around the door of the music-room, where she saw William absorbed in a copy of Maclaurin's *Fluxions*. She wrung her hands. If his hobby persisted in overriding his work, they could lose more students. Mrs Colebrook would come out of her fit of pique eventually, but her departure threatened more serious losses. Between conducting at the Octagon and teaching music, William earned a comfortable four hundred pounds each month. If his reputation faltered, it could change quickly.

Mrs Colebrook had, it seemed, forgiven William, for at their next performance, she greeted the siblings as usual. But Caroline was certain, listening to her friend's chatter blend with the conversation around the rooms, that while the widow had once imagined standing by William's side as his musical star ascended, the lady certainly did not wish to encourage anything astronomical.

Because she could not expect another letter from William for at least a few days, Caroline accepted Mrs Colebrook's invitation to take a stroll following tea.

'It *is* up the hill, Miss Herschel, but a sight worth seeing. With you so near, I'm surprised you didn't realise it was complete,' Mrs Colebrook said.

Caroline shook her head. 'I'm afraid we've been spending more of the moonlight hours out of doors than the sunlit ones,' she said, following Mrs Colebrook from the Rooms into the crisp autumn air. She ignored her companion's disdainful look. Pulling their shawls close, the ladies made their way past the townhouses of the King's Circus, past rows of trees with leaves turning a burnished gold, and uphill to the fields which commanded the grandest views of the city. Another sweep of Palladian architecture stood above the fields.

'Just look, Miss Herschel.' Mrs Colebrook gestured as if she had built it herself. 'The Crescent is finally complete. These shall be the most sought-after homes in Bath.' She tilted her head confidentially. 'I understand the Linley family have already purchased number eleven.'

Caroline felt a thread of jealousy tug in her breast. Miss Elizabeth Linley was an acclaimed singer and local beauty. These were the most elegant homes in the city – perhaps in all of England, for what Caroline had seen in London was comparatively decadent. Those buildings were not like The Crescent, with its rich austerity and sun-flooded facades. But what right had she to envy Miss Linley, when, if not for William, she would still be in dismal Hanover?

A clap of hands made Caroline turn. A group of schoolboys ran about the sloping field just below the new houses, with two ladies attempting to shepherd them. Mrs Colebrook fell silent and followed Caroline's gaze.

'Gather round,' one teacher called. 'Now, George, you must be the Sun,' she said, positioning one boy. 'There's a good lad.' She instructed the other six boys to stand around the first. 'And you must be the planets.'

'I'm Earth! Ooh, let me be Earth,' one shouted, throwing his hand into the air.

'Jupiter! I'm King of the Gods!' squealed another.

A bustle broke out.

The ladies watched as the teacher aligned the boys in their respective places from the sun – Mercury, Venus, Earth, Mars, Jupiter, Saturn.

'I'm burning – I'm the Sun!' the first boy announced, and the others giggled.

'Now,' said the teacher, standing back to appraise her work, 'we need –'

'—the Moon, of course,' Caroline murmured. Mrs Colebook shot her a glance.

'The moon,' Caroline repeated, more loudly. The teacher nearest them looked up in surprise.

'And what about the various comets and asteroids, which fly about? You will have them, will you not?' Caroline continued, overwhelmed with the thought that if William had been there, he could not have resisted saying the same. 'Have you explained that the orbits are elliptical, not circular? And what of the other planetary satellites – have you no more pupils to fill these spaces?' She resisted the desire to say they had left out a planet – William's planet, the Georgian Star. But this recent discovery had yet to become common knowledge.

The teacher began to turn crimson. 'I – I beg your pardon, Miss, I only…'

'No, my dear, we beg *your* pardon,' Mrs Colebrook burst in, grasping Caroline's arm and tugging her indelicately away. 'You enjoy your game – rather, your lesson. It's coming along wonderfully. Please forgive my friend – her head is in the heavens!'

'I want to be an asteroid!' cried a boy, dancing into the circle and smacking another boy in the head. 'Boom, crash!' The second boy began to cry.

'What's an elliptical? How do we do an elliptical?' yelled another, spinning until he fell to the grass.

With Mrs Colebrook leading in a huff, Caroline peeped over her shoulder, suppressing a giggle as the 'heavenly' bodies in the Human Orrery began to degenerate into general disarray.

Chapter 5

The following day, Caroline set about dressing a brace of pigeons in preparation for Alexander's return. It was odd to be left alone for such a stretch of time, and though William, for his kind attention and interesting conversation, had always been her favourite brother, Caroline found herself looking forward to Alexander's company.

He overflowed with news from London, and his gossip, like Mrs Colebrook's, washed past Caroline without her absorbing much. She waited for the words to abate before presenting William's letter.

'Oh ho, what a clever brother we have, Caroline,' Alexander said, helping himself to more wine. 'A cut-out of Saturn indeed. But no news from the King.'

'No,' Caroline said, 'not yet. But do you think he will stay, Alex? Remain in Windsor, and send for us? Are these to be our last weeks in Bath?' She prodded a rosemary sprig on her plate.

'*Us?*' Alexander lowered his fork. The word had arrested his full attention. 'Sister, I don't intend to go to Windsor, no matter how great the King's favour. I'm sorry if I made you think I would.'

Caroline cleared her throat of suddenly over-dry meat and took a swallow of wine. It felt as if she'd peeked through a telescope, for nothing appeared as it had a moment before.

'But…we three have done everything together,' she said, shaking her head. 'I only – I presumed…'

'I'm sorry, Caroline. It's a fair assumption, but William wishes this change. Not I. Teaching music is too fulfilling, too lucrative, to trade in for the lathe. I'll remain in Bath, and travel to London – perhaps if the time is right, I shall move nearer to Windsor, teach more in London,' he added, patting her hand in vague reassurance. 'It's like that night when we were children, and Father took you and William out to stargaze. Remember? I chose to stay inside, in the warm.' He returned to his meal.

She fixed her mind's eye, and the memory sharpened into focus. Isaac crouched in the crisp winter night, a warm arm wrapped around her. William stood by her side.
Holding her cloak tight, Caroline tried not to shiver in the chill air. She gazed at the heavens as Father pointed past the sloping rooftops and crowded chimneystacks to describe points of light.

Here were the Twins; there, the Great Bear. The Seven Sisters were a faint cluster. How different life must be with seven sisters, rather than four brothers! Jacob, Alexander, and of course baby Dietrich, had all remained indoors by the fire, but William and Caroline had cried '*Jah*!' to their father's offer of a tour of the night sky.

Caroline found her eye constantly returning to a point of light that outshone all others, whisking across the sky as if a painter had dipped his brush in light and smudged a streak of it beside the moon.

'Father, what is that?'

'That, Lina, is a comet.'

Comet. This was different from the other stars. Caroline forgot about the cold.

'It is like a travelling star,' Father said, 'which leaves a trail of stardust in its wake.'

One day, Caroline thought, she too would travel.

Watery lamplight spoiled the darkness as Frau Herschel bore down on them.

'*Carolina*! Bedtime!'

With great reluctance, Caroline left the safe space between her father and William to heed her mother's order.

'...Do you recall that night, Sister?' Alexander's voice, heavy with fatigue, brought her back to the present. 'Even then you were happy to stand outside assisting William in his astronomical studies. At what age?'

'Nine years old,' she murmured. 'That short time when William and Father came home between battles.' She did not wish to dwell on the times when they both were absent. Such as now.

She rose from the table, gathering the empty plates. 'Go rest, Brother. You've had a long journey.'

The memory Alexander had prompted was the earliest she had of purposely looking up to the heavens. But it was not the grandest. Sloshing a bucket of washing water into the kitchen basin, Caroline was reminded of a much larger tub of water that Isaac had set up in order to watch the Great Eclipse.

He'd gathered the family. Frau Herschel was impatient; Jacob was absent; Dietrich was more interested in a butterfly that had landed on the sun-warmed cobblestones. But Caroline, just home from school and breathless with haste, leaned eagerly over the tub.

'The Great Eclipse,' Father announced, rubbing his hands together, 'is meant to take place in just minutes. Now, don't look at the sun – don't, don't!' he yelped as both Dietrich and Caroline turned their heads skywards. Caroline blinked, wincing, as spots sprang to her vision.

'*Listen*, children!' Father said, exasperated. 'Shortly, the moon will pass between Sun and Earth, obscuring the Sun.'

Dietrich splashed his fingers in the tub and Father *tutted*. 'Dietrich, please don't touch the water. We want it smooth as a mirror in order to watch. It will protect our eyes. It damages our vision to look at the Sun directly. You've both just tested this theory.'

Frau Herschel put a restraining hand on Dietrich's shoulder and he danced with impatience.

'The sky will darken,' their father continued, 'but you need not fear – as the moon continues on its orbit, the sun will shine again, just as before.'

'Oh,' Caroline gasped. The sky had indeed begun to darken, and a black sliver was creeping towards the wavering reflection of the sun. Dietrich fell quiet, watching, and even their mother looked on now with interest.

'Marvellous, just marvellous,' Isaac muttered.

The family held a unified breath as darkness slid across the sun's face, and daylight was cloaked in tarnished silver. The moon sat directly in front of the sun, a ring of blackness rimmed with fierce light, reminding Caroline of some great cosmic version of the shadow-puppets Dietrich played at, making shapes in front of a lantern with his fingers. The obstructed beam, with the light behind, projected the shapes onto wherever the candlelight shone. This meant that there should be a great circular shadow pouring down onto the Earth, and Caroline gave a little shudder as she realised that shadow must be the darkness in which they stood. The *brightest* blackness she had ever seen trembled as a gust of wind danced across the surface of the water.

As they peered into the tub, the moon carried along its path, and, five minutes later, slid off the face of the sun. Silent, they watched it go.

'Where on Earth *is* everyone?'

The familiar voice, and Caroline's shriek of excitement, broke the spell.

'William!'

There he was, striding into the courtyard. She threw herself into her brother's arms as Mother, Father, and Dietrich all fell upon him with hugs and cries of joy. After a few moments of tumult, Frau Herschel stood back, holding her son at arm's length.

'*What*, child, have you got round your neck?'

'It's the English style, Mother,' William said, laughing. 'They call it a *cravat*.' He toyed with the cloth at his neck. 'Which is of course French, but then they copy all their styles from the French.' He chuckled and moved to clap his father on the back. 'Observing the Great Eclipse I see, Father?'

'Why of course, my boy,' Isaac said, throwing an arm around his son's shoulder. 'Did you know, I was only yesterday reading a pamphlet on the phenomenon…'

The shifting of the water in the kitchen basin calmed as Caroline stilled her hands, and the shadows on the rippled surface smoothed into her silhouette.

That had been one of the most joyous of William's visits, and one of the cruellest. By chance, his departure had been scheduled at the very time of her Confirmation. The blast of the post waggon leaving Hanover, bearing him away once again, shattered her thoughts during the church ceremony like a hand dashing the smooth surface of water.

Chapter 6

A fortnight before he was summoned to Windsor, William conducted a concert at St Margaret's Chapel. Caroline sang, and together, they performed a well-received duet. But as the evening wore on, William's tempo faltered. Caroline overheard approving murmurs, as she always did, at his musical versatility. But she also heard something new: that this might be Mr Herschel's last public performance. Confusion revolved in Caroline's head, made worse when William rushed away, whispering that it was a clear night, and he had to get to his telescope.

That same evening, she'd had a conversation she'd barely had time to mull over.

'You're an ornament to the stage, Miss Herschel,' a tall gentleman said, after introducing himself as Mr Bellows. 'I should like you to sing in my upcoming festival at Birmingham.'

Caroline could only wonder why her brother had disappeared so swiftly.

'Thank you, Sir,' she said, hesitating. 'May I ask if my brother shall be conducting?'

Mr Bellows looked surprised. "Well no, Miss, that would be my privilege. I'm visiting Bath looking for a few more singers, such as yourself. The fee would cover all of your expenses and more. It's a highly respected festival of music, I can assure you.'

She glanced past Mr Bellows, hoping she would see William chatting with some of the Octagon's more important patrons. He was nowhere to be seen.

'Thank you for taking the time to speak to me,' she said, curtseying to her guest. 'But I'm afraid I must go find my brother.'

'But, wouldn't you…?'

She didn't stay to hear the rest.

The offer only began to come clear in her mind days later, when William demoted her from first soprano to second. Miss Scott had to be given the place, he explained, for reasons of social delicacy – namely, her father's generous donation to the Octagon. Caroline asked after Mr Bellows, but he had booked his singers and left for London. She was trying not to think about Miss Scott's unwarranted privileges when William's second letter arrived.

His Majesty King George III had offered William a position as King's Astronomer. This was entirely separate, William wrote, from Maskelyne's post of Astronomer Royal at Greenwich, which focused on navigational astronomy for the Royal Navy. This new appointment would make William independent of his reliance upon music once and for all. He would be able to carry on his astronomical work freely. He would have to reside near Windsor Castle: that way, the Royal family could summon him for astronomical education when they pleased, or call on him at home, where he could host viewings using the large telescopes. William had already rented a house in the nearby village of Slough, with a fine garden for observing. As for Caroline: she was officially named his assistant.

Slumping into the slipper chair, Caroline bumped the oboe and it fell to the floor with an echoing thud. She left it.

If fate was written in the stars, then her musical path ended here. Alexander would remain in Bath, but she would go. She was too close: locked into William's orbit, his influence overwhelmed the trajectory of her own desires.

Looking around the room at the comforting curves of the musical instruments, the gleaming bodies which she had polished, and the fine gut strings which she had tuned, Caroline let out a perfectly pitched sigh.

She would go to Slough. She would become an assistant astronomer.

Even Alexander's usual light-heartedness was affected by the gravity of the mood that settled over the house at New King Street: a mood Caroline knew was entirely of her making. In silence, he helped her pack, and, in silence, she fretted. William wasn't there: she didn't have to pretend to be pleased.

One thing that vexed her was the implication that she, as William's assistant, would have to play host to a myriad of Royal guests, as if she and her brother were some curio spectacle. The great twenty-foot telescope William had built in their garden in Bath attracted a stream of visitors, but at least that had been under their control.

Making the great twenty-foot had been a spectacle of its own.

'Five hundred and thirty-eight pounds of metal!' came Alexander's cry from the workshop. Caroline gulped cool night air. Their friend Watson had ushered her outdoors, the heat and stench being 'too much'. He would not say 'too much for a lady,' for they had spent days side-by-side, sieving dry horse dung for speculum moulds.

'Five hundred and thirty-seven point nine,' came William's reply.

'Pedant!' Watson jested.

There was a pause, and Caroline knew the men were pouring metal into the mould. This was a critical moment. Upon the first trial, the mirror had flowed like liquid silver, but cracked as it cooled. William made adjustments to the recipe, and here they were, in a second attempt. Caroline wiped sweat and dirt – perhaps dung; she didn't dare think on it – from her face.

Silence.

Then a great rumbling arose from the workroom, and Caroline would later swear she saw the roof sway. Shouts, followed by a great explosion, and her brothers shot from the doorway in a cloud of smoke and rubble. They lay on the ground, bewildered and soot-streaked, as Caroline rushed to pull them further from the building, where dust and mortar flew.

'What happened?' she shouted over the din.

'The furnace – leaked,' gasped Alexander. 'The flagstones – blew up – as the metal hit the floor.'

William lay staring at the sky in dismay. The rumbling ceased and the dust began to settle.

'Watson – where is he?' Caroline cried.

'Here,' came their friend's shaky reply from the far end of the garden. 'I dashed through the kitchen door – thank goodness there are two exits.' He limped over, face streaked black.

'You are unhurt?' Caroline asked.

'It's nothing – a small blow to the foot,' he assured her. 'I daresay we escaped easily.' He ran his hands through his dust-whitened hair and looked at the smoking workshop. They all stared in silence.

'Well lads,' Watson finally announced to his friends lying on the grass, 'I suppose we must let the metal run its course and then have another go. What do you say?'

Caroline tensed as she waited for her brothers to answer. Would this failure put an end to their madness? Did she want it to?

'...We'll need to reinforce the furnace,' Alexander finally ventured.

'Of course,' William broke in. 'And we can recover most of the metal, I'm sure.'

By his side, Alexander nodded.

William sat up, gesturing to the wooden frame awaiting its telescope. 'We've come this far. Next time, I *know* we will succeed.'

Caroline coughed, and then began to giggle, in dismay or relief she did not know. It was better than sobbing, anyhow. Alexander's chuckle followed, and soon they were all on the grass, holding their sides with mirth, and any onlooker might have thought them a group of confirmed lunatics, mad with the influence of the moon.

Once the mirror was smelted – for the next attempt *had* been a success – the twenty-foot telescope was erected in the garden, and the flow of visitors increased.

Their visitors at Windsor would be, of course, of a much higher rank than most of their guests in Bath. But then, their most famous guest at New King Street had been a person of no small standing.

One evening, William had told Caroline that an esteemed party would pay a call to see the telescopes. However, in his absent-mindedness, he had misplaced the card from the messenger who had requested the visit. They didn't know who would call, or at what time. Feeling unprepared and out of sorts, Caroline rushed about the house, ensuring all was tidy as could be. She wore one of her finer dresses of white cotton muslin, and tied her long hair back with a blue ribbon. With some dismay, she'd discovered her brother in the garden, hunched over a telescope trained on the setting sun.

'William, I wish you would wash up before our guests arrive, and please change into another shirt. It's freshly pressed on your bed. We don't know who to expect.'

'Solar observation, Lina: I've devised an excellent contraption for it,' William replied, straightening his back and grinning. His dark hair was wild, and she could tell he'd been running his hands through it in one of his fits of invention.

'See? I've built a slot just here for this glass jug, and I'm pouring in different fluids to test the various powers of filtration. Galileo was clever enough not to strain his eyes at the sun; I think we can manage the same, don't you?'

He bent, returning to the scope.

'Galileo still ended his days as a blind man,' Caroline grumbled. 'William, our guests arrive in a few hours to view the night telescopes.' She looked at his smudged frock coat and dirty sleeves. 'Please wash up. And stop pulling your hair.'

William waved her close.

'Look, Lina, this works mighty well as a filter.'

With a sigh, Caroline stepped forward to peer through the sun-scope. A dark red blob swam into view. It took her a moment to accept that she was truly looking at the sun. She had looked at stars before, yes, but her hand was at the pen much more often than her eye was at the scope, jotting notes for William as he looked into the heavens. And this was so different. Patches of darkness wavered, suspended in the orb, which swirled enigmatically with heat and light. Perhaps if they tried –

'Very nice,' she acquiesced, halting her wandering thoughts. William was rapt in his observations; she must not become so too, or they would never get anything done. Besides, if she was distracted by solar observations as well as assisting William at his stellar endeavours, when would they *ever* sleep? Mornings were the only times they were able to rest.

'Please wash your face as well – how did you get soot on your nose?' She pulled her kerchief from her pocket, spat, and reached for him, but he fended her off.

'I will wash, Lina – but don't you see? I've used claret for the filter – good claret. The better the fluid, it seems, the better the filter.'

Until he'd mentioned the claret, Caroline had not taken note of the open bottle sitting on the grass beside the telescope.

'How much claret did you use?' she asked, looking first at the bottle, then, through narrowed eyes, at her brother. 'Have you been drinking it as well?'

'Not much,' he said quickly, running his hands through his hair. He shuffled his boot in the grass.

Caroline closed her eyes and took a deep, slow breath.

'Promise me you'll tidy up before our guests arrive, Brother.'

'Of course,' William said, pressing his eye once more to the scope.

Corking the bottle of claret, Caroline stalked indoors.

Shortly after dark, she opened the door to greet their guests. One woman stood out immediately – the same lady Mrs Colebrook had pointed out in London. The Duchess of Devonshire stood on their doorstep. All of the ladies in the group wore towering hair in the latest fashion, with feathered hats perched on top. But the Duchess's hair was higher, her hat brim wider, her feathers flouncier. Her gown of blue silk shimmered in the candlelight.

Caroline led the guests into the garden and introduced William, though he needed little introduction. Most had heard him perform at the Octagon, but they had come, these most fashionable people of society, to see her brother not at the organ or violin, but at his telescopes. The Duchess demonstrated genuine wit and curiosity, asking William questions about his work. This interest in stargazing, from the likes of Dr Watson and his Royal Society, to the celebrated Duchess, startled Caroline.

*

Now, packing away sheet after sheet of musical scores, unsure of when, if ever, they would be played again, Caroline wondered whether astronomy was second to music after all.

Chapter 7

The house William had rented was a disaster. Alexander quietly pointed out that their older brother only worked diligently at projects of interest to him, and Caroline was grateful when Alex agreed to stay for a week to help put things in order.

They needed as many hands as could be spared. Yes, the garden behind their new home was vast, and good for viewing. Yes, the stables could be converted into a workshop to grind mirrors and build telescope tubes. Yes, the garden sheds could house the lathe and smelting cauldron for specula.

But the *house*.

The roof leaked. The former occupants had left a good deal of clutter, subsequently taken up by a family of dormice on the first floor and a family of pigeons on the second. A pile of bricks sat in the parlour where a wall needed repairing. Yes, the house in Slough was much larger than the one in Bath, but then, there was that much more to clean. When Alexander almost fell down a well hidden beneath weeds, Caroline discovered that even the garden needed to be dug out and landscaped.

As she struggled to fit the crockery into the pantry, a plate slipped from Caroline's hand and cracked in two on the flagstones.

'I'm off, Lina.' William's call made her grind her teeth. *He* was not concerned with the pantry.

'The King wishes to see the seven-foot reflector, so I've sent it ahead to be set up. I shall be spending a great deal of time, you understand, at the Queen's Lodge, for His Majesty wishes me to show him his planet again, and other stellar objects of interest.' He looked around, as if only just noticing the disastrous state of the room in which he stood. 'You…do your best to make heads or tails of this…I know you will, Lina.' The excitement returned to his expression, and he was gone to meet the King.

Wondering where Alexander had got to, and whether he was making himself useful, Caroline marched out to the garden.

'Already at the lathe, Alex?' she said in despair. 'I need your help removing the dormice.'

He stopped the lathe and brushed off the wooden object he'd been turning.

'Why? Have they refused to pay rent?'

Caroline tossed up her hands.

'Don't fret, Sister,' he said, 'we'll sort things out. Here – I was making a present for you. A moving-in gift.' He handed her the object, warm off the lathe. 'Now, I shall evict the mice.' He made a little bow.

'Oh – thank you,' Caroline said, surprised. The piece of wood was glossy black, and fitted comfortably in her palm. 'What is it?'

'A worry-bead,' Alexander called, making his way toward the house. 'To stop you rubbing your hands raw.'

She smiled wryly, rolled the bead in her palm, and dropped it into the deep pocket of her skirt. It was a thoughtful gift, but she would need more than a worry-bead to endure the sacrifices William asked of her.

Finally, with William at Court, the house settled, and Alexander returned home to Bath, Caroline was left to sweep the skies. One merit of the ramshackle house in Slough was a small, two-storey brick cottage beside the main house, with a flight of stairs leading to a rooftop terrace. Caroline had claimed the ivy-covered building, fitting out the two upstairs rooms as lodgings. Her telescope – a small, lightweight reflector made especially for her – had pride of place on the roof.

In Bath, Caroline rarely had the opportunity to sweep the heavens, for she was too busy sweeping the house, assisting with rehearsals at the Octagon, or taking notes for William as he viewed the sky. But one week, when her brother was confined to bed with fever, and the skies were clear, he'd begged her to trade her calculations for his observations.

At first, she protested. She could write down his dictation without error, but stargaze herself?

'Don't be ridiculous, Lina.' William waved off her concerns. 'Keep the scope trained to the meridian. Move it slowly in vertical sweeps, making note of anything unusual as you go. Read the stars as you read my sheets of music.' He paused for breath, and Caroline offered a cool cloth for his forehead.

'As the night passes,' he continued, taking the cloth, 'the sky, moving with the Earth's rotation, will move slowly through your field of vision. On a good night, you might complete a full two degrees of arc.' He closed his eyes wearily, and Caroline knew she could not refuse.

After sharing her garret in Hanover with baby Dietrich, and the attic room in Bath with Alexander, her 'cottage' was the first space she'd ever had to herself. Her rooms were sparsely furnished: in one sat her small trunk from Hanover, alongside a bed and the slipper chair from New King Street. In the adjoining room stood a dressing table, wardrobe, and an oak wash stand with a porcelain basin and ewer – chipped, but serviceable. Each room had one square window overlooking the garden and workshops to the back, and, to the front, the small patch of lawn between the house and the road.

Downstairs, William had begun to hang their many maps, graphs, and charts. He'd stored a pile of boxes of astronomical notes and sketches there as well, and they'd begun to half-jokingly call it the Muniment Room. But their main work was done in the parlour of the big house, and it was here that Caroline's standing desk had been set up; here, she copied William's notes that had not yet been stored away.

If she ignored the enquiring neighbours; if she forgot the thieving servants she'd already had to sack; if she shrugged off the butcher overcharging her because she was a newcomer; if she excused the workmen for loafing about the garden in the name of making repairs; if she did not think of William dining with the great and good at Windsor Castle; if she put off the piles of washing, darning, and note-copying…if Caroline muffled the din of distractions and stepped onto her terrace to look through her sweeping telescope, then yes, she enjoyed her role as astronomical assistant. Her reflector was a seated design, so she could perch on a stool and put her eye to the lens. There, she learned to love the silence. Warmed from without by layers of woollen petticoats and shawls, and from within by a dish of hot, sweet coffee, she would put her good eye to the reflector, and sit, alone, beneath the sky.

Chapter 8

William returned with many interesting pieces of news, but there was only one message Caroline managed to take in.

'The Queen wants to meet *me*?' she asked, confounded. 'But why?'

'You, dear sister, are a phenomenon,' William said, waltzing Caroline around the parlour. 'A *lady astronomer*.' He wriggled his eyebrows. 'What newly-discovered species is this?'

Frowning, Caroline pulled away. 'I do not want to be paraded around like some curiosity!'

William *tutted*. 'It's not that way, Sister, I swear. It's a great honour, and yes, they are curious, but they aren't fools – especially not the Queen. You'll like her.'

The atmosphere at Court was much like that of the grandest venues in Bath at the height of the season. It had never been a social stage on which Caroline wished to take centre. In the dazzling rooms of Windsor Castle, William introduced her to a score of people, the names and faces of whom passed in a blur.

Throughout her life, most of the people Caroline encountered failed to hold her interest. They might be kind or rude, handsome or unattractive, witty or boring, but she rarely found her attention captured. William had so many exciting ideas that her mind was taken up with thoughts of their work. She had necessarily endured Mrs Colebrook for many years, but after adjusting to the English language, Caroline had rarely felt enlightened in the woman's company.

Walking around the ballroom, her arm in William's, Caroline noticed that people mingled and gathered into groups, much as they did in the New Assembly Rooms, to discuss the latest news. She curtsied politely when William introduced her to a gentleman he had met on a previous visit. William and his acquaintance fell into conversation over the latest troubles the King suffered at the hands of the upstarts in his American Colonies. As they talked, Caroline's ear was drawn to the richly accented voice of a man nearby.

'Oui, *L'histoire Céleste Française* is progressing, Monsieur, but I fear you will not see it in print for some time.'

The title sounded familiar. Caroline drifted nearer.

'Work at the Paris Observatory continues successfully, *oui* – ah,' and here, a warm laugh, 'but I should not say too much, for His Highness has called in his own *astro-no-mers*.'

The last word was rolled out, making Caroline smile. Competition for claiming new comets and nebulae was both friendly and fierce. Dr Maskelyne insisted upon confirming and announcing discoveries with great speed, in order to beat Messier at his game.

But Maskelyne had described the esteemed French comet-hunter, and this man speaking of astronomy did not appear to be the same person. Like Charles Messier, this man appeared to be William's age, perhaps older. But Maskelyne had said that the French astronomer was no taller than the Emperor Napoleon, and he insisted on wearing a powdered wig in public, despite the fact that the fashion was going out. This man was tall, and wore a waistcoat and jacket of embroidered brocade. He wore no wig; in fact, his head was bald, round and smooth as any planetary object. His eyebrows were angular, expressive; his eyes the iciest blue Caroline had ever seen. It was almost unnerving to look at them, and she wondered if he used drops of belladonna to intensify the colour. She had heard Frenchmen were given to vanity.

'Pardonnez-moi, *mademoiselle*, have I the pleasure of your acquaintance?'

Startled, Caroline blinked, realising the question was directed at her. She dipped into a deep curtsey in an attempt to hide her blush, and stayed low, hoping William would come to her rescue. After a moment, when the curtsey should have passed, the man reached out and lifted her chin, raising her. His blue eyes met hers, his forehead shone like a full moon, and every thought flew from her head save the touch of his cool fingertips.

The hand dropped, and he smiled.

'Allow me to introduce myself, *mademoiselle*. Jérôme de Lalande, astronomer at the Observatory at Paris.'

The clamor of music and conversation, the perfumed heat of the candlelit room, suddenly overwhelmed Caroline, and her vision spun. Lalande's smile vanished and he grasped her arm in concern.

'You are unwell, Miss. Please, allow me.' He guided her to a chaise near a window, gesturing to a servant. Moments later, Caroline was settled into the thick upholstery with a glass of port. She took a sip, steadying herself, and smiled at Lalande, who hovered nearby. The draught creeping through the window frame was a relief from the great blaze in each of the room's many fireplaces. It seemed the Court did not wish to feel the early winter chill.

'*Merci*, Monsieur. I'm afraid I was overcome with…' Caroline paused, unsure what had caused the spell of dizziness. She tried again. 'It is my first visit to Court, and I admit I am dazzled.'

'Ah,' Lalande said, looking relieved. 'It *is* impressive if you have not attended before. But –' he paused.

'Yes?' Caroline said.

'Well, not as impressive, Mademoiselle, as the French Court,' he said with a wistful smile. He leaned in, eyes bright. 'But many here regard Windsor's equivalent, the Palace of Versailles, as a place of excess.'

Caroline's own eyes grew wide, but she did not have the chance to hear more.

'Lina, Sister, there you are,' William's relieved voice interrupted. 'I couldn't for the life of me discover where you'd hidden yourself, and we mustn't keep the Queen waiting. Oh,' he said, realising she was engaged. 'Why, *bonjour, Monsieur Lalande!*' he shook the man's hand warmly. '*Je vois que vous avez rencontré ma sœur. Magnifique. S'il vous plaît, pardonnez-nous.* Now then, Lina?'

Feeling the blush rise once more in her cheeks as William announced she was his sister, revealing their astronomical connection, Caroline stood, nodded to Lalande, and followed William away. She glanced back only once, but her gaze met those arresting eyes. He stared as if he'd made the most enchanting discovery of his life.

Caroline hardly had time to suffer nerves before being introduced to the Queen. She felt calm, despite the fact that the room seemed even more full of courtiers than the Ballroom. The Queen had a serenity and grace befitting her position. Caroline found herself summoned from a curtsey for a second time that evening, this time meeting the gentle grey gaze of the Queen.

'I hope, Miss Herschel, that you are not overwhelmed by the glitter of mirror and chandelier, after spending so much time out of doors,' the Queen said, as if privy to news of Caroline's earlier spell.

'Thank you, Your Highness,' Caroline murmured. 'I own it is quite a change from sweeping the garden.'

The Queen paused. 'You sweep the garden, Miss Herschel?'

As this exchange was whispered throughout the room, a collective chuckle arose.

'Oh, no,' Caroline hastened to clarify. It seemed the topic of astronomy was misunderstood at Windsor. Now, she supposed, was her opportunity to enlighten the Court. Wasn't that William's role, and hers?

'Sweeping with telescopes, Madame.' She held her arm out, sighted along it, and slowly swept it up and down. 'It is the method with which we chart the skies.'

Another titter rose from the company, but the Queen appeared genuinely interested.

'I think I begin to understand,' she said, gesturing for Caroline to walk with her. 'Tell me more, Miss Herschel.'

After a rich meal of roast fowl, herbed breads, and sweetmeats, the party dispersed to play at whist, stroll on the terraces, or retire to sofas with drinks in hand. Caroline's palate danced: on most days, out of habit, frugality, and convenience, she ate porridge.

Some of the Queen's ladies in waiting encouraged her to join them at cards, but she insisted she would rather watch. Gambling was not a hobby she intended to take up, especially as William's income was half what it had been, and their expenses more dear than in Bath. She settled onto an embroidered stool near the card table. Bored, she began to wonder if the sky was clear and if they had missed a good night for viewing. Her own name interrupted her thoughts.

'...Miss Herschel? Pardon me. Is it truly you?' The woman folded her lace fan and clasped Caroline's hand in soft-gloved palms. Caroline smiled, trying not to betray her confusion.

'Oh, you do not remember me,' the woman said, 'but it is such a joy to see you, and who would believe it – Caroline Herschel and Emmeline Beckedorff together, in Windsor Castle, in *England*.'

Caroline gasped. 'Emmeline?'

The woman let out a girlish giggle as she pulled another stool close and perched upon it. 'Yes! And both of us looking quite different.'

'But the last time we met…' Caroline said, thinking, '…must have been a score of years ago.'

'Longer. At Confirmation,' Emmeline said, nodding, her dark curls dancing. 'All of those tedious lessons. And then at the ceremony, the trumpet outside startled you so, you began to weep, you poor thing. Do you recall?'

'I wish I could not,' Caroline said tightly, the painful memories sparring with the joy of seeing her friend again.

Another lady who had been attending the Queen earlier rustled over, her skirts flowing like the liquid silver William used in his specula.

'Forgive my intrusion, ladies. Madame Beckedorff, would you kindly introduce me?'

Emmeline rose and curtsied. 'My pleasure. Miss Herschel, this is Miss Burney. We attend the Queen together. Do join us, Miss Burney.'

'Oh,' the lady said, waving her hand and settling into a chair. 'Dear Emmeline, do call me Fanny. You must as well, Miss Herschel, if you wish.' Her voice lowered. 'When we are not amongst the Clowns and Courtiers, that is.' She laughed, and turned an inquisitive gaze on Caroline. 'Now, Miss Herschel, I hear great things about the telescope at – is it Observatory House?'

'I have not heard it called thus.' Caroline admitted, shy in the presence of such congenial company. 'But I doubt there is any other house which could bear the name.'

'That is what they have taken to calling it at Court,' Emmeline confirmed.

'Yes,' Fanny said, 'and whilst your brother –' She paused to flash Emmeline a look. Emmeline snapped open her fan and began to peer around the room with great interest.

'—has been enthralling his audiences here at Windsor, there is talk of making outings to the house. I understand there are great telescopes to be seen, much larger than those Mr Herschel brings here.'

'Well,' Caroline said, hesitating. She wished she were better informed. Had William failed to tell her this? Or had she been too distracted by the prospect of meeting the Queen to pay attention? 'It is our duty to entertain and educate the Royal Family, Miss, and I suppose that includes whomever they wish to invite,' she said. 'We do have some impressive telescopes, the largest being the twenty-foot,' she added, hoping to satisfy Miss Burney's curiosity. 'But they are meant to be looked *through* more than to be looked *at*.'

'Splendid!' Fanny said, clapping her hands together. 'I believe you've inspired the Queen herself with a wish to peer into the heavens.'

'Oh yes,' Emmeline added, lowering her fan. 'It sounds as though she will not be disappointed.'

Chapter 9

The grand visit to Observatory House would not occur, it seemed, for some months, for as the nights grew longer and darker, the Royal Family made it clear that they had no interest in standing outdoors in the cold. William was freed from his obligations at Court, and he and Caroline resumed their observations.

The *Georgium Sidus* was now called 'Uranus'. It had done its job of gaining William patronage from the King, and the planet required a name in the traditional, mythological style. As astronomer's assistant, Caroline could explain the discovery of the new planet as needed, but most frequently, she took notes on William's observations of Mars, double stars, nebulous clusters, and whatever else took his fancy.

One evening, as Caroline fastened the last of her many wool petticoats, a mighty crash from the garden sent her running downstairs. She had known it would collapse, that rickety frame supporting the twenty-foot! It had never been properly reassembled after the move. The viewer would be perched on beams sixteen feet off the ground – and the viewer could only be one person.

'William!' she cried, throwing herself at the wreckage of splintered wood. Two men who helped at the lathe worked to pull her brother free. The winter wind snapped around them. Why couldn't he have waited for the gusts to die down?

'I'm fine, fine, thank you,' William gasped as they lifted him from the heap. He brushed splinters from his hair. 'Oh God, the mirror! Is it hurt?' He began wrenching broken planks aside.

'Bring the neighbours, Lina, it's too heavy to lift free.'

Caroline hesitated. 'William…you could have *died*. My concern is for *you*—'

'I'm fine!" He snapped. 'What if the mirror is damaged?'

Caroline stepped back as if he'd slapped her.

William hesitated, his look softening into one of pleading. 'Lina – you understand how much we went through to make this. You understand how important it is.'

Caroline reached into her pocket and grasped the worry-bead. 'Of course, Brother. I'll fetch them.' At least they'd been living at Obs House long enough that the neighbours wouldn't be too surprised at the request.

Several hours later, it was determined that the great mirror – five hundred and thirty-seven point nine pounds of metal – was unharmed. It leant against one of the garden sheds, innocently reflecting nearby trees. The wind had died at last.

'The carpenters will have a great deal to contend with tomorrow,' William said, eyeing the wrecked frame. 'Pity. Such a fine evening, too. Barely any moon to brighten the sky.'

Caroline nodded. It would be good, for once, to retreat indoors to the fireside.

'I suppose,' William said, 'for the remainder of the night, our observations will have to be with the seven-foot.'

Later, as William called out his notes, Caroline's usually smooth script wavered as she concentrated on keeping quill to paper.

As winter progressed, the twenty-foot was repaired and a proper viewing gallery constructed, with improvements. To support the tube, William devised a mechanism around it, like the frame of a hoop skirt. A system of pulleys, cords and hooks enabled a few men to spin the whole contraption to face whichever direction William wished, and to raise and lower the tube's height with ease. The only hooks they could find that fit the gears were those the butcher used for hanging meat, and the metal glinted from recesses in the base, where the cords were pulled taut, securing the operation. A set of wheels beneath the base allowed free movement – though not so free the wind could blow it apart.

They pressed on with observations as the nights grew bitterly cold, for the colder the air, the clearer the heavens. Caroline knitted fingerless gloves so they could be nimble yet protected from the sharp night winds. She wore so many petticoats she looked like a tiered cake. One night, moving to jot an instruction from William, Caroline's pen hit the bottle with a crack. The ink had frozen. It became necessary, on the coldest of nights, to sit at the open window, a fire burning in the hearth, her ears perked for William's shouted instructions.

Both siblings slept long into the mornings, and by midday, both were up and to their tasks. Caroline oversaw the maid's cooking and housework, then retired to her standing desk to respond to letters and copy William's scientific papers. Only rain drove her brother indoors - William was outside on even the coldest days, instructing the workmen at his latest project. He'd hired so many men, he now required them to wear numbers pinned to their coats, and simply shouted directions at a number rather than keep track of names. This was, he explained, for the sake of efficiency, and especially useful when they needed assistants in the dark of night; the white-painted numbers were far more recognisable than individual features.

And they would soon need more hands for their astronomical work, for William had embarked upon building an even larger telescope. Caroline wondered if the fall from the twenty-foot hadn't addled her brother's brain, for he had drawn up plans for one double the size.

'The mirror will be nearly fifty inches in diameter: forty-nine and a half,' William said, pointing to the drawing rolled out on the dining table. He leaned over the table, analyzing his sketches. 'The tube will be forty feet in length.'

The polished mahogany table had seen more star charts and diagrams than formal suppers. The long-case clock ticked from its place against the wall.

'That will be nearly large enough to stand in,' Caroline said, trying to keep the skepticism from her voice.

'For you, my dear *little* sister, it will be,' William said with a smile, 'though I'm afraid it won't carry you to the moon – only your sight.'

'And this will enable us to see twice as far, Brother?' Caroline asked, calculations running through her mind as she peered at the sketches.

'That's the plan, Lina,' William said, 'to see farther into space than anyone before me.'

'But William,' Caroline said, reaching up to squeeze his shoulder, 'you already have.'

'And I must continue to do so,' he said, sitting down suddenly. 'For how can one measure success, Lina, but to continually aspire to greater achievements?' He shoved his hands through his hair, elbows on the table. 'The heavens prompt *so many questions* which no one has yet been able to answer.' He turned and took her hand, his eyes dark, worry mapped across his face.

With a shock, she saw how fully he'd devoted his life to his dreams and inventions. Teaching and composing had never held this weight. He was in competition – with himself.

'You are already a success, Brother,' Caroline said, hoping with all her heart that he could have a fraction of the belief in himself that she had in him. 'And you will continue to be one.'

Chapter 10

On New Year's Eve, Caroline insisted on clearing the dining table of all work-related clutter, and laid out supper for two. Alexander would have joined them had he not recently become engaged to one of his music pupils, a lady called Jane. All he had written of her thus far was that she was 'sweet and unassuming' – and that her father had insisted Alex pass the holidays with their family.

Caroline maintained the barest communication with her mother and Jacob in Hanover, but William kept in better contact, sometimes sending money home. They'd received a curt 'to your health' from Frau Herschel leading up to the holidays, written in Jacob's hand. They'd had charming letters from friends including Watson, the Maskelynes, Miss Burney and Emmeline Beckedorff.

After their meal, and sharing the letters, Caroline mixed a hot gin punch, and William sat himself at the spinet. He was just ending a song, his long fingers still hovering above the keys, when he glanced out the window.

'Good heavens, it's cleared! We must call for the assistants,' he cried, leaving the spinet and hurrying into the kitchen, where one of the assistants was playing cards with the maid. They had no particular place to be, and William had agreed that they could remain at Obs House over Christmas and enjoy their time in leisure. This, it seemed, he'd forgotten.

'Timothy, I'm afraid there's been a change of plan. I need you to fetch the others from the village and hurry back as quickly as you can,' William said. 'Send Erik out, too, if it will help,' he added, gesturing to the maid's son, who sat by the hearth sleepily patting one of the barn cats. Neither Timothy nor Erik looked pleased at the prospect of stirring, as Caroline hurriedly followed her brother from one room to the next.

'I insist they have a hot drink before they go,' she said, pouring cups of punch for all present.

'*Prost*,' William said, raising his cup, and the others followed suit. 'To a productive New Year.' He drained the drink, thumped the cup on the table, and nodded. 'Now, make haste! We haven't viewed for days, and the clouds are clearing.'

As William buttoned his greatcoat, Caroline dashed out to the cottage to pull on her extra petticoats and shawls. It was a frosty night, and she shivered as she pulled on her layers. Her eagerness to get some work done was countered by the warm, pleasant company they'd been enjoying. Couldn't William rest, just once? If only this had been a profession, not a passion: a career, not a hobby. Then he mightn't love it so much. Then he could let himself enjoy other aspects of living, as he used to.

Surfaces gleamed with ice, and her leather shoes slid on the flagstones as she headed to the garden. The assistants were gathering, and William was already up in the viewing gallery of the twenty-foot. He would not wait for all of the men – not everyone would heed his summons on this of all nights.

'Rotate me round to the East,' William cried, 'Quickly now, Lina, make an adjustment of point-eight degrees to the lateral motion.'

Caroline rushed to carry out the instruction. She climbed over a wooden beam. Just before she reached the central mechanism, her feet flew from beneath her. She fell, a red-hot poker searing into her thigh.

'Make haste!' William shouted.

Caroline's vision spun. 'I –' she gasped.

'Lina!' The voice was impatient.

'I am hooked…' she struggled to find her voice. '*I am hooked!*'

Figures swarmed towards her in the dark. *Take care,* she wanted to cry, *these wicked meat-hooks, so useful in holding the ropes* – but her voice was carried off on a wave of pain. A gentle hand was upon her shoulder, and she made out a number in the dark – Timothy.

'Miss Herschel, what have ye done?' His voice was filled with worry.

'I am hooked,' she whimpered, fighting tears.

'Lina! What the Devil happened?' William's voice was much closer now – he was upon them. As they lifted her free, Caroline let out a strangled scream, her petticoats soaking warm with blood.

They laid her on a settee in the drawing room and one of the workmen hurried to bring his wife, who had some knowledge of medicinal herbs. The injury was far up Caroline's right thigh; none of the men could examine her – it would be scandalous. But the herb-woman, left alone in the room with Caroline, paled at the first glimpse of the wound.

'Oh, Miss, I'm sorry – I cannot –' she groaned, rushing from the room, leaving her basket of remedies behind.

Biting her lip, Caroline dragged the basket closer. A cup of forgotten gin punch, now cold, remained on the table beside her, and she swallowed the rest of it down. Tears streamed down her cheeks as she splashed the torn flesh with aquabaseda. She bit her lip and trembled, the pain shooting like a lightning bolt through her bones. After a pause, she gathered a breath, wrapped a bandage around her leg and yanked it tight as she could. Then she fainted against the cushions.

*

'Two ounces,' Dr Lind looked at her in disbelief. 'You left nearly *two ounces* of flesh behind on that hook, your brother said. And you nursed yourself?'

Caroline fixed her gaze on the scrubbed wooden floor. It had been over a month since the accident. She only had a faint ache, and a slight limp, but finally, at William's insistence, she'd called for the doctor to examine the gash in her thigh.

'Do you realise, my dear, that a soldier with such a wound would have been entitled to six weeks in hospital?'

'No,' she said, her gaze shifting from the floor to her hands in her lap.

'You *must* take care,' the old doctor said helplessly. 'It is healing well, but could easily become inflamed. *Life-threatening*, Miss Herschel. I should have seen you straight away. Now,' he said, rummaging in his bag and handing her a few small items, 'here is ointment, which you must apply after you wash, and lint, to pack around the leg, and then wrap it gently as you have been doing. It should help assist the healing process.'

'Thank you,' Caroline said, humbled by his concern. She had, perhaps, treated the accident too lightly. But to think of the state of the house, of their work, if she were consigned to bed for six weeks!

Dr Lind shook his head. 'Was your assistance missed?' he asked, after a pause.

Caroline raised her eyes to meet his. 'I didn't go outdoors for a few nights following the incident, as the weather was so poor,' she said, 'but once the skies cleared, we were both back at the scopes.'

There was another pause, and Caroline thought the doctor might have more to say, might, perhaps, congratulate her on her bravery and commitment.

'Tell your brother that I trust he's taken measures to cover those hooks,' Dr Lind said, sighing. 'And *do* take care, Miss Herschel.'

Despite the doctor's warnings, Caroline was determined to prove that she was not diminished by the injury, that she did not require dainty-gloved mollycoddling, and that no one could fulfill William's needs for an assistant better than she. She made a point of standing outside to take notes in the weeks following her appointment with Dr Lind, insisting that she could better hear William's instructions in the open air. Besides, the coldest time of year was past. The season was pushing on to that time before spring when all turned to damp, and mud jostled beside ice on the lawn.

Chapter 11

The thaw of early spring coaxed forth Royals as well as crocus buds: with the days once again lengthening, William was recalled to Windsor. This time, Caroline was relieved rather than dismayed by his absence, for she worried he'd become too immersed in his experiments, and he needed the company of society to set him right again. The onions had confirmed it.

One evening, as the assistants pushed the twenty-foot on its revolving stand to a new position, the reek of onions assaulted Caroline's nose. Though the thick warmth of the horses hung round the stables; though the workmen smelled of sweat and tobacco, and the workshop of sawdust and metal, this was odd. She realised with a start that the scent was coming from above her.

'William?' Caroline called up from her little table with its shaded lamp. 'Why do I smell onions?'

A chuckle drifted through the dark.

'Keeps away the ague, sister!' William called. There was a shuffle, then a thump beside her. She leant over and plucked up half an onion, its papery skin crinkling beneath her fingertips, its face seeping juice.

'Rub it thoroughly on your exposed skin and it will keep away the chill,' William said. He fell silent, back to his sweeps.

'Will keep away everything an' everyone,' one of the assistants muttered, and there was another chuckle. Caroline smiled.

'Aye, a mug of ale each night will keep off the ague as well,' a voice answered, 'withou' being so unpleasant.'

Murmured agreement followed, and one whisper that dashed the smile from her lips. '*Lunatic.*'

She tossed the onion into the hedge.

'Thank you, Brother – I'll risk it for now,' she called. 'I feel in quite good health.'

It wasn't how she'd have wished it, but when William fell ill with fever not long after starting with the onions, she was able to convince him to leave off the unpleasant exercise.

'I have been proven wrong,' William said as she mopped his forehead with a cool cloth. 'A successful experiment. What shall I try next?'

'You needn't worry about that, Brother,' Caroline said, grateful she could answer. 'The King has sent for you, and once you recover, you're wanted back at Court. As for the remedy, I have it from Dr Lind, and it's no experiment: two ounces of red bark, abstain from solid food besides mutton broth and bread, wine negus and toast. Now you mustn't argue with that!'

'No, Lina, I shan't,' William said weakly.

Lunatic: the whispered word, uttered in the darkness of the onion-scented night, haunted Caroline. She reached into her pocket and grasped her worry-bead, which rested just above the ugly scar on her thigh. Both she and William were guilty of spending too much time living in their own heads, with little thought for their bodies. If it *was* Lunacy, perhaps the workmen were right to be concerned, for it must be contagious. Caroline never thought she'd endure standing out on a frosty night taking notes for William, but she'd grown to actually enjoy it.

She enjoyed it so much, that when William recovered and left for Court, she once again set up her lightweight reflecting telescope on the flat roof of her cottage so she could sweep the skies herself. The telescope had been packed away downstairs all winter while she'd taken notes for William. He sought nebulae and comets – changeable objects of interest that might not have been spotted before. These were elusive, and he'd begun to focus on his favourite stellar objects: double stars.

Caroline would never forget the first time William described them to her. The siblings were still living in Bath, and were working over a breakfast of porridge and astronomical notes. He'd become enchanted with the doubles, and at the same time, he'd begun pushing his musical duties to the side.

'Many of the stars we see are not one, but two. With great enough magnification, we can see that what appears to be a single star is frequently coupled with a smaller, fainter star. One of the pair burns brighter, Lina, so without looking closely, a person might not know the other star existed at all. But it is my guess that one cannot exist without the other.'

There was a familiar intensity in William's eyes as he paused to take a spoonful of porridge. It was the mathematician in him, the philosopher, the architect, the artist – all worked within the whirring gears of his mind to piece together these ideas. She'd transcribe the thoughts into one of his scientific papers eventually, she was certain.

'It is my guess that they are necessarily double – binary sidereal systems orbiting under mutual gravitational attraction. They are in pairs, these double stars; they cannot exist separately. Am I right, Lina? Is one forever fated to exist only alongside the other?'

She waited, knowing his habit of rhetoric. He wasn't expecting her to speak; he was working out these thoughts for himself, and she happened to be – was fortunate enough to be – there.

'Only time,' he finally said, 'and precise observations, to see if there is an effect of parallax, will help me answer the question.'

Content to leave the abstractions to William, who could, if pressed, sketch charts and diagrams into the air, Caroline resumed her simple sweeps. It was likely that anything she saw would either be of little use to her brother, or already marked by Charles Messier. But she was alone in the house, no one needed her, and she relished her chance at the scope.

She slowly manoeuvred the sweeper, pausing every so often to make a note in her book. Adjusting her vision from the darkness of space to the dim flicker of candlelight and back again took time, but she had time to spare.

Without the squeaks and groans from the rotating twenty-foot, the murmurs from the workmen, or William's shouted instructions, Caroline could make out delicate nocturnal sounds: a breeze rustling the dry-clinging leaves yet to be shaken off branches and replaced with new; soft cooing from a pair of doves in the eaves below; the mellow breathing of horses in the stables.

And footsteps.

Her ears pricked, and she stilled, feeling both hidden and exposed: a prowler would be unlikely to look up to the cottage roof, and might try the house or stables if intent on theft, but an astronomical visitor would look for William on the twenty-foot, or for Caroline here on the roof. With that logic, if she were seen, it would be by a welcome guest, and if she wasn't, she might have time to do something about it.

The footsteps stopped near the stables, and then there was a shout.

'*Alors*, a lady on the roof? *Bonsoir, madamoiselle.*'

The warm voice brought to mind a noisy room, strong port, and startling blue eyes. Lalande.

Caroline smoothed her hair and skirts and turned towards the stairs, but he was already making his way up. Reaching the roof, he bowed, and Caroline could guess he was smiling in the dark. She, too, could not suppress a smile as the moonlight danced off his bald, pale pate.

'Not like the Paris Observatory, I fear, Monsieur Lalande?' Caroline asked. She was tempted to unveil the lamp – such a dark setting, and just the two of them, might have been odd – but for the circumstances, and her night vision –

'Keep it dark, *mademoiselle*,' Lalande said, seeing her hesitantly reach for the lamp. 'The night vision, it is precious. And no, not like Paris, just as Windsor is not like Versailles.' He paused. 'But they have their unique charms.'

Caroline was grateful for the dark, which hid her blush.

'I'm afraid William is not in, Sir,' she said, 'but in fact at Court. I'm sorry you missed him.'

'Ah,' Lalande said quietly, 'I must apologise for turning up without notice, for I have recently arrived from France, and wished to call here before making my way to Windsor. I do not mean to inconvenience you.'

'Not at all,' Caroline said, frustrated that she might disappoint him. 'I'll do my best to show you the telescopes, Monsieur, but I'm afraid I won't provide explanations half as detailed as William's. I understand if you prefer to visit another time, when he is here.'

In a burst of enthusiasm, Lalande took up her hand and kissed it. The darkness concealed her startled look.

'*Merci, merci*, I would greatly enjoy a tour, if it does not trouble you,' Lalande said. 'Your explanations will be a delight. Above all, I am glad to see you in your true habitat, and thriving. I heard of your terrible accident…'

Caroline showed Lalande the reflector before they made their way down to the twenty-foot. She pointed out the covers for the hooks, and described what she could recall of the incident. She told him of the old frame for the twenty-foot, William's fall, his double stars, the assistants, and making the specula. She pointed out the giant tube of the forty-foot, which was slowly taking shape in a corner of the garden, and explained the difficulty their carpenter had in bending the thing, until William devised a series of wooden hoops to support it. Clouds rolled in, and she invited Lalande for coffee.

'Ah, *café*, an astronomer's drink,' Lalande said, settling into an armchair by the fireside. 'Fortune is at my side, allowing me to interrupt your work on a cloudy evening.'

She answered his questions about the mirrors, the lenses and levers, the mishaps and experiments, their methods and theories. His accent wrapped around each topic like gilt paper around a gift. Caroline reveled in untying each piece of their conversation, in seeing what it contained. There was no competition: only the thrill of discovery. For a time, William had won on that score, identifying Uranus as a planet. Caroline knew that the fanfare following the discovery, which set William on his path as an astronomer, was a great challenge to live up to, not least for William himself. Perhaps such success, so early in his career, had skewed his expectations. Lalande agreed about the pleasures and pressures of their work. What in William's career could outshine such a thing as the discovery of a new planet?

Lalande brimmed with enthusiasm about the achievements Caroline described, and simmered with frustration about the difficulties she confided, as if they were his own. In a way, they were – Lalande had as much right to the sky, knew it as intimately, as she and William.

Refreshed by the coffee, they traversed the garden together, their quiet voices casting vapour into the night air. As Lalande looked through the seven-foot and into space, Caroline was pleased that he agreed with the superiority of William's scopes. With her brother absent, she need not play the assistant, and found she could answer Lalande's questions; equal his observations.

As they discussed a calculation, she showed him the multiplication table that she kept in her pocket – she found it impossible to commit the tables to memory, and keeping the chart alongside her worry-bead allowed her to carry out the conversions William needed.

They discussed William's theories about binary stars and parallax, measuring the relationship of the stars with the earth. She showed Lalande the illustration William was working on, which looked like a great black swarm of bees stretching across a piece of parchment, with two arms reaching away to the right side.

'This is his visualisation of the heavens – the structure of the entire night sky,' Caroline explained. 'We are used to thinking of it as a flat plane; even the old idea of being within a crystalline sphere is usually laid out like a pancake above our heads. But William says we must begin to conceive of ourselves in three dimensions, floating in a vast ocean of space.'

'As if we swim through the air?' Lalande asked.

Caroline nodded, smiled. 'Something like that.' It was an impossible problem. 'He measures each star, and plots its point, and marks it. I believe my brother is able to see things in a way most people cannot.'

Lalande nodded. 'A curse and a blessing. And you have to interpret it, comprehend it.'

'Oh, hardly,' Caroline demurred.

'Truly,' Lalande insisted. 'Every day you must understand his genius. I have read your brother's published papers, and I admire his approach – he thinks widely, imagines what is possible. He stretches his mind to encompass what *could be*, despite criticism and doubt. So much of what we know today contradicts what people once accepted as fact. Take the Copernican theory of the universe, *par example*! Can you imagine believing Earth at the centre?

Caroline shook her head, chuckling. 'Or that the Milky Way is a backbone, holding up the sky?'

Lalande smiled. 'Why, your brother's ideas could change scientific thinking just as dramatically.'

Caroline agreed. It seemed they shared a similar view of the cosmos.

Chapter 12

William returned from Windsor with the news that Miss Beckedorff and Miss Burney simply could not wait for the Queen to come to Observatory House. The ladies were to pay a visit only a few days hence. Caroline flew into action, sending Erik to the market so his mother might plan a proper meal, ordering the workmen to clear the garden of assorted debris which might catch on fine hems or slippers, and delving into her own clothes trunk to unearth her finer dresses. Waistlines had crept even higher, William described, so they were just beneath the bust, but Caroline had to see it before she could alter any gowns. With a flash of nostalgia for Mrs Colebrook's interference, she resigned herself to last season's style.

'Oh, but it's wondrous,' Miss Burney gasped as Caroline led them towards the forty-foot tube.

'It's our biggest yet,' Caroline said. That much was clear, but she hesitated to go into too much mathematical detail, for fear of boring her friends. She was learning to judge her audience, and rather than presenting all the facts, waited to be asked questions. If a guest was interested, he was welcome to learn more. If not, she wouldn't burden him – or her – with information. Most people seemed satisfied with the surface of things. The awe the tube evoked, while genuine, was nothing compared to what it would be like to look through the completed telescope – something most people would not go out of their way to do.

'Delightful,' Emmeline said, eyes wide. Again, Caroline bit her tongue. Telescopes were amazing technological constructions – sculptural, even, but not delightful. They were also fragile, frustrating, and demanding in their needs for precision and maintenance. Oh, what one knew when one's life was shuttled into a wooden tube!

William invited first Miss Burney, then Miss Beckedorff, to walk through the tube. Miss Burney exited, mouth agape.

'But it holds me without the slightest inconvenience – I could be wearing feathers and a bell hoop and remain upright and undisturbed!'

William laughed. 'A slight exaggeration, Miss, but not far off the mark.'

Miss Beckedorff hesitated at the far end of the tube, and William hurried forward to offer his hand. She thanked him, smiling as she stepped down onto the grass.

'If only one could exit on the Moon,' she said, looking up at William.

'Ah, perhaps you would see a colony of the men who live there,' William answered. Emmeline's eyebrows shot up and Caroline stifled a giggle. *That* was one theory best left to the breakfast table. She hurried to invite the ladies to the cottage, then the rooftop, to show off her sweeper.

'William, please tell Hannah we'll soon be in to dine,' she called as she led the ladies up the stairs.

'It must be such a pleasure to work as your brother's assistant,' Miss Burney sighed.

They had reached the roof and looked out onto an illuminated landscape, a view Caroline did not often see. In the distance, across rolling fields, the impressive bulk of Windsor Castle's north face looked out from its rocky seat. The Thames sparkled in the softening light of late afternoon, and white fluffs of newborn lambs dotted the surrounding fields, the stockier cumulus shapes of their mothers never far off. The view from the front of Observatory House was clear, with only a short track before it met the road. Turning to look out over the stables and work-sheds, Caroline recalled with sadness one of the first alterations William had made to their new home.

The one-acre garden had swiftly been transformed into a busy workspace of sheds, muddy boot-prints, and discarded piles of metal and wood. The sounds of hammering, sawing and grinding cut through the hollyhocks and bluebells, which would bloom again in spring. A great crash overwhelmed the din as a large old tree came down.

'All of them, William? Must we bring all of the trees down?'

'Don't be foolish, Lina, of course they must all go,' William said, waving her aside as she followed him past the stables. He was deeply involved in renovations, and her arrival with Alex seemed to distract rather than assist William as she'd hoped.

'But…they provide such lovely shade,' she protested. 'And they're so *old*, William.' The ancient elms had clearly existed long before the house, meandering haphazardly about the field and creating a scattered woodland around the sheds. It only seemed fair that they should accommodate the trees, but William evidently saw little use in it.

'Lina, you know we're moving the twenty-foot, and there will be other telescopes before long. There is not time to consider shade or longevity.' He scoffed. 'After all, we work in the dark – we don't need shade.' He waved his hands towards the men chopping wood. 'And I can't have any of those damned oaks blocking my view of the sky.'

'Elms, William,' Caroline called as he made his way over another fallen tree and into the house.

He could only look up, her brother. Most people only saw things at eye-level, but he couldn't see below the level of the sky. She wrung her hands as a workman shouted a warning, and flinched as another tree fell to the earth with a crash.

'They're elms.'

'…Miss Herschel? Caroline?' Her friend's voice returned Caroline to the present.

'I'm sorry,' Caroline said, shaking her head. 'I lost myself for a moment.'

'It's no surprise, with the work you do,' Emmeline said gently. 'So demanding, and left on your own so often.'

'I don't mind that,' Caroline said. 'And to answer you, Miss Burney, it is a pleasure to work with William, yes, and often a challenge, too.' She paused, wishing to turn the conversation elsewhere. 'But – he mentioned your novels. I'm afraid I haven't read them, and I'm sorry. But allow me to say it's quite an achievement. You must be proud.'

'Oh, pooh,' Miss Burney waved off the compliment, her brown curls bouncing fiercely around her face. 'Call me Fanny, firstly, my dear. Secondly, thank you for being honest. I am *most pleased* you haven't read my novels, and that you tell me so. Most people who praise my books have never read them either! I'd rather they not read them and think I have talent, than read them and know I have none!' She burst out laughing and Caroline couldn't help but smile at her enthusiasm.

'Don't be silly, Fanny,' Emmeline broke in. 'You are *both* skilled – I can say so, for I knew Caroline when we were quite young, and she was skilled then, too. And I have read every one of Fanny's novels.' She nodded firmly.

'But your work, Caroline, it's so fresh, so interesting,' Fanny said. 'I should *so* like to write about it. What a novel your story would make, my dear.'

'I'm not so sure about that,' Caroline demurred. 'Perhaps if you wrote it.'

Fanny grinned, and pressed Caroline's hand. 'Of course, you will have to teach me which end of the telescope to look through.'

'And I shall be the first to read it,' Emmeline said, reaching to take their hands. Together, they looked out upon the darkening shape of Windsor Castle, the stone of its western side gilded by copper fingers of sunset.

Soon after, Erik called them to dine, and they were so engaged in conversation for the rest of the evening that, much to Caroline's relief, William wasn't able to get another word in about men living on the moon.

Chapter 13

Spring bloomed into shorter, lighter nights, and William was called to the Castle more and more often. As the season stretched into summer, Caroline discarded her extra shawls and petticoats, and spent more time sitting at her reflector. Meanwhile, the forty-foot frame was well under construction. The great tube, awaiting its housing, lay like an ancient dolmen in the grass, with vines and insects making a home of it. The Queen had officially expressed an interest in seeing the large telescopes, and plans were finally stirring for a Royal outing to Obs House.

August brought a long-awaited visit from Alexander. Caroline was curious to meet his fiancée, Jane, but she'd fallen ill and was unable to travel.

'I would have stayed with her,' Alex explained, his eyes full of concern, 'but she said it was a minor ailment, and she insisted I come. She knows I haven't seen you both for quite some time, and when William asked me to help with this special order – well, I knew a reunion was overdue.' He reached back and smoothed his long hair, now fashioned into a plait.

'She sounds a selfless, amiable woman, brother,' William said, 'and we're very pleased for you.'

Caroline nodded as she refilled their wine glasses.

'And she approves of you travelling with me to the Continent – an amiable woman indeed,' William continued. 'One might almost think it's worth having a wife.' He winked at Alex.

'William!' Caroline admonished. He mustn't trifle with their brother that way. It was perfectly acceptable that Alexander wished to marry, just as she'd accepted she never would. She precisely recalled the one cruel thing her father had ever said to her: 'Lina, as you are neither handsome nor rich, I feel it is my duty to caution you against all thoughts of marriage, for it is unlikely that anyone will make you an offer.'

Hard words, though in them, her father had intended protection. He had been right. William's offer to rescue her from Hanover had been the best, the only, offer she'd had, and now nearing her mid-thirties, she was well into spinsterhood.

'We're very happy for you and Jane, Alex,' Caroline said, moving to clear the plates from their meal. 'And we'll be glad to meet her when she's fit to visit. Now, you both must finish packing, for the coach comes early.'

The King had commissioned five ten-foot telescopes. He was sending them as gifts to heads of state throughout Europe. With the scopes came the brothers, who would instruct on the set-up and operation of the fine instruments. Their first stop was Göttingen, after which they would pay a visit to Frau Herschel, not far away.

Caroline left instructions for the morning meal with the maid, and went to the sitting room to check the fire. She absently rolled the worry-bead in her palm, a habit that had indeed stopped her wringing her hands. Reaching for the bead in her pocket was a gesture she no longer noticed.

'Is that your worry-bead, Caroline?' Alexander asked, passing with a pile of manuscripts in the crook of his arm.

She smiled and held it out to him. The dark wood had a warm patina from all the handling. 'Indeed, Brother, and I must thank you for it – it did the trick. My hands are chapped from work and cold, but not from fretting.'

'And what did you put in it?' Alexander asked, tossing it into the air and catching it smoothly.

'What do you mean?' Caroline asked.

'Here,' Alex said, laying the papers on a chair and twisting the wooden egg with both hands. It came apart in two halves, which he turned towards the firelight, revealing a small hollow within. He chuckled at the look of surprise on his sister's face.

'You mean to tell me you never opened it?'

'Goodness, I never noticed the seam,' Caroline said, taking the pieces and examining them in disbelief. 'How clever! You always were best at the lathe.'

'Well, now you know,' Alexander said with a smile, 'so you may put something of great worth, and small size, inside.'

'Yes,' Caroline murmured, screwing the bead together, watching the seam disappear. 'I will.'

'I must bring these to William,' Alex said, collecting the manuscripts. 'And we'll say farewell in the morning.'

This time, her brothers' departure – especially William's – did not bring up painful memories, for this time, Caroline had a sense of purpose. After the carriage rattled away with her brothers and their expensive cargo, Caroline went to her cottage rooms and tucked a lock of William's hair into the worry-bead: a dark lock he'd given her years ago, which she kept in her jewellery box. She wound it tight and put it in the equally dark nut of wood, and slipped it into her pocket. The lock didn't betray a hint of the grey that now glinted from the hairs on William's head in abundance. This small piece of him might aid her sweeps while he was away.

She made a slow tour of the grounds, enjoying temporary ownership of the estate. The forty-foot was nearly ready to be mounted in its frame, but William had decided they should wait, and have the Queen's visit take place while it was still on the ground. It delighted guests to walk through the telescope tube. They would make a garden party of it, and invite their neighbours as well as the Queen's entourage. The house was in good order, and because the brothers had spent the past month on the King's commission, there were, unusually, no papers to copy, and only letters to answer. The workshop was a minor disaster: the brothers had hurried to finish the ten-footers before their journey, but Caroline gladly locked the doors to the main shed, leaving it to be sorted when they returned.

The sky that evening was peppered with clouds, and though she doubted her chances of seeing anything at all, Caroline was eager to try. After eating her porridge and tidying her letters, she headed to the rooftop to sweep the skies. She would try to see what she could find, and if the clouds proved too dense, she could move indoors to work on calculations. There were always plenty to check, and check again. William and Nevil Maskelyne had praised her error-free work, and she was not about to give them cause for complaint.

The shuffling of the horses and chirruping of night birds tempted Caroline to listen out for a soft footstep in the garden. It was foolish, but she hoped to meet with Lalande again. She knew he'd returned to Paris, but this hadn't stopped him writing letters, both to her and to William, with more thoughts and questions, to which she gladly responded. His enthusiasm and intellect set her mind whirring, and she found herself missing not William's, but Lalande's company.

As Caroline moved the sweeper slowly along the meridian, a faint blur caught her attention. As she concentrated on it, thoughts of anyone and anything else flew from her mind.

She looked just to the side of the object, rather than directly at it. The construction of the human eye was such that one could see better in the dark from the sides of one's eye rather than the centre. She wasn't certain how it worked, but it did, just as adjusting her eyes to the dark helped with night-vision, and she could see more sharply through the telescope when no light distracted her. Viewing the blurry object was almost an exercise in flirtation – not trying overly hard to see it actually helped her see it better. Caroline was grateful not to need to explain this to Emmeline or Fanny, for she was sure they wouldn't understand. They might only accuse her of flirting with stars rather than men. The latter was something she didn't know how to do at all.

After a few long minutes, as the sky turned above her – she reminded herself that she was in fact on the Earth, turning *through* the sky, but it never felt that way – she shifted her attention to her notebook and began to sketch the object in relation to the constellations nearest it. Over an hour passed before she could precisely ascertain the direction in which it moved, and she thought of the stories in the sky as she began to trace its path.

Caroline had first spotted the blur near the tail of the Great Bear, Ursa Major. Myth had it that the bear was once a beautiful woman after whom the god Zeus lusted. His jealous wife turned the girl into a bear, and to save her from being shot by a hunter, Zeus swung her up into the night sky by her tail, stretching it long.

She watched the object move through Ursa Major towards Coma Berenices: Berenice's Hair. This group of stars, an asterism, was considered the tuft on the end of the lion's tail in the constellation Leo. Myth claimed that Queen Berenice of Egypt agreed to sacrifice her long blond hair to Aphrodite if King Ptolemy returned safely from a wartime campaign. When this came to pass, the long braid of hair was laid in the temple of the goddess.

The next morning, it was gone. The King's astronomer was summoned to explain to the furious royal couple why the precious hair had disappeared, and the clever man saved his own skin by announcing that the goddess was so pleased, she'd placed the braid in the heavens.

The object – a *comet* – of significance in mapping the heavens – was making its way from a constellation of a god to one of a goddess, from male to female. Now *this* was something to tell Fanny Burney.

Later, inside her cottage rooms, Caroline scribbled in her notebook. 'This evening I saw an object which I believe will prove tomorrow night to be a Comet.'

The following day, the second of August, Caroline spun her worry-bead in her fingers and calculated nebulae, impatient for night to fall. An oppressive rain threatened to spoil any opportunity for viewing, but it cleared around midnight and Caroline immediately climbed to the rooftop.

She focused her reflector on constellation Coma Berenices, and searched.

Yes: it was a comet.

After assuring herself she knew what she saw, she hurried indoors and began writing to the natural philosophers and friends to whom she'd written, on William's behalf, so many times before. She started with Lalande, telling him of both the comet, and the garden party, and then wrote to Maskelyne, Banks, Watson and Aubert. She wanted to write to her brothers, but did not know precisely when or where a letter would find them.

She resolved to wait until they returned. These letters were different – not from Caroline working as her brother's assistant, but from Caroline making a discovery in her own right. She had spotted the comet and recognised it for what it was, and now she would claim it by alerting those learned men. And she would hope that Messier had not seen it first.

With her brothers gone for some weeks on the Continent, there was time for Caroline's letters to make their way to London, Greenwich, and beyond. Maskelyne replied swiftly, confirming her sighting, and followed up with a note from France: Messier had not sighted the comet. It was Caroline's.

The letter that pleased her most, however, was addressed not to her, but to the *'astronome célèbre'* at Observatory House. Lalande managed to carry off his flirtatiousness with a grace and wit that Caroline enjoyed. From anyone else she would have been embarrassed, but she flushed with pleasure as she read his praise. He was certain she would find more comets, and rival even Messier at his hunting. Through her weeks of solitude, each time Caroline thought of something she might have asked or shared with William, she found herself instead wondering what Lalande's response would have been. She was delighted to read his postscript: he would come to the garden party.

The news of the comet also brought a flood of visitors, as if they'd rediscovered the chance to visit the telescopes. This time, however, everyone asked for the Lady Astronomer, and Caroline was obliged to carry her reflector down to the garden and show off her comet. She was uncertain of this new celebrity, used to William answering questions while she directed people on the use of the scope's eyepiece. Now, she had to play both astronomer and assistant.

One night just before her brothers' return, Caroline was in the garden sweeping when she heard a commotion from the other side of the house.

'See? I told you it was round back!'

'Gracious, it's like the Colossus of Rhodes, that hulk in the dark!'

'That'll be the best telescope in the world when it's done, I daresay.'

'It'll damn well be the largest.'

'You don't suppose Herschel is, ahem, *compensa* –'

'Good evening, gentlemen,' Caroline called as she unveiled her lamp. The comments stopped abruptly and she curtseyed. 'Welcome to Observatory House. Ah, dear Watson!' she cried, recognising her friend. He clasped her hand.

'Miss Herschel, forgive our intrusion,' Watson said, making a small bow. 'My friends from the Royal Society insisted on coming to meet the Lady Astronomer.' He introduced his companions one by one. 'Miss Herschel, may I present Mr Joseph Banks and Mr Alexander Aubert.'

Caroline curtseyed again, feeling as if she were back onstage in Bath. Joseph Banks – why, he was President of the Royal Society!

'It's an honour to meet you, gentlemen, especially to have the opportunity to put faces to names,' she said. 'As we've shared many letters.'

'Miss Herschel, your comet was beautifully drawn,' Mr Banks said, 'very accurate. Commendable work.'

'Thank you,' Caroline murmured, and not for the first time, she was pleased that the dark hid her blush.

'We had to see the comet-seeker as well as the comet,' Mr Aubert said. 'You see, my dear, we understand the fortitude required in stargazing.'

'Not mere stargazing, man!' Watson interjected.

'No indeed,' Caroline said, 'I call it sweeping the skies, or minding the heavens – but perhaps that is too domestic for your tastes?'

The men broke into chuckles.

'And your brother, Miss? Is he about?' Banks asked.

'I'm afraid he's in Göttingen, Sir, with our brother Alexander. They are delivering new ten-foot reflectors from His Highness.'

'And why are you not at Windsor Castle, Miss?' Aubert asked. 'Surely they want for clever women in that company!'

'She's too busy discovering comets, can't you see that?' Watson replied. 'And here we are, distracting her from her work.'

Banks hissed and tapped his companion's foot with his walking stick. Caroline hid a smile, enjoying their banter.

'Oh, it's no trouble at all,' she said, waving a hand. She turned to Aubert. 'And to answer you, Sir, I haven't much taste for crowds, though I have been invited, and perhaps shall return to Court when William also returns.'

'Yes, you must,' Banks encouraged. 'Your comet is all the gossip at Windsor.'

Caroline invited the gentlemen into the parlour and served claret while telling the story of William, the sun-scope, and the Duchess of Devonshire. The men were in stitches over William's single-mindedness with the claret.

'What a creative mind,' Banks exclaimed, when Caroline described her brother's use of liquid filters.

They asked to view Caroline's comet using her sweeper, and returned to the garden.

'Historic, you know,' Aubert announced, his eye to the scope.

Caroline completed the visit with a detailed tour of the other scopes, outlining the plans for completion of the forty-foot. She indulged in technical language, knowing they would understand.

William and Alexander returned to find Observatory House a much busier place than they'd left it. Their joy over Caroline's discovery was countered with sombre tidings of Frau Herschel's death. The brothers had arrived in Hanover to find their mother in a final illness, under the care of their youngest brother Dietrich and his growing family.

They agreed it was providential to have been present at Frau Herschel's deathbed, but privately Caroline wondered if the old woman hadn't waited until her sons had arrived before dying out of pure spite. Her mother would not have heard news of her comet; would never know how far her daughter had soared beyond those low, servile tasks. Mourning their mother's death made it inappropriate to celebrate Caroline's success; Frau Herschel was bitter and cruel even in the afterlife, tarnishing the glory of her daughter's work.

William insisted that they would celebrate the comet at the garden party, just as they would celebrate the forty-foot telescope. Alexander went home to Jane, and Caroline focused on plans to host the King and Queen.

'You did not wish to return to the Castle, Lina,' William said, 'so it seems the Castle will come to you.'

Chapter 14

Princess Augusta signed the Visitor's Book with a flourish before following her mother into the garden. Caroline trailed after them, delighted with all the names in the book. The late summer day was sunny and clear, and no one was more relieved than she. Tables had been arranged indoors and out; the doors to the parlour were thrown wide open, and the Court, members of the Royal Society, and neighbours to Observatory House flowed throughout the grounds. Ladies stood around the garden, blooming beneath parasols and hats; men in linen suits hovered about them. Shawls were discarded and waistcoat buttons loosened in the sun. Punch was served along with cakes, cold beef, smoked fish, fruit, and fresh breads.

For the occasion, Caroline had treated herself to a new dress of floating muslin sprigged with pink and green flower buds that would have made Miss Carsten proud. She wore a bonnet with an arching straw brim that shaded her face and held her hair out of the way. Her cheeks were scrubbed; her fingernails clean. When helping William prepare his suit for the party, she'd discovered the fit was too snug, and she'd altered it. The flesh at his waist and jowls was spreading gradually, just as his hair was becoming more brightly streaked with silver.

The King, whose moods were known to be turbulent at best, announced his delight in sharing a day with fellow Hanoverians. He looked content as he examined the various astronomical instruments around the garden, and Caroline was relieved, well aware that his patronage relied upon his pleasure. It was their good fortune to have a King who loved astronomy, and who shared connections with their homeland. Meanwhile, William had captured the ear of a group of guests by describing his fancy that the universe would one day break apart.

'But fret not!' he hastened to add as several ladies gasped and looked pale. 'It shall not happen for thousands and thousands of years – perhaps more. None of us will be around to see it.'

The true attraction, however, was not the Lady Astronomer, nor her brother, nor the twenty-foot. It was the completed tube of the giant forty-foot telescope. Emmeline and Fanny had been the first at Court to see it, and had done a good job of drumming up excitement when they had brought their tales back to Windsor Castle.

'This shall be marked on the new Ordnance Survey map of the neighbourhood, I'll see to it,' the Duke of York announced to Watson and Aubert, as Fanny once again described to the Princesses her adventure through the unfinished tube.

'Oh, may we go through it?' Princess Charlotte asked William. This was what they all had come for. In its present form, it was more like a child's climbing-toy than a tool for astronomy, but that was what William had cleverly planned. The tale of the Royal Family having stood in the very telescope with which he would make his greatest discoveries would ring in the halls of Windsor for years to come.

First William stepped into the tube. Then, calling in an echoing voice, he lent a hand to the Queen. Powdered, with a frilled neckline far more formal than any garden party required, she delicately stepped within. Cheers went up, and soon a whole train of folk tromped and rattled through the telescope, with William, like the Pied Piper, at the fore. Caroline knew how sturdy the structure was – if it could bear the weight of the mirror waiting to go into it, it could bear the weight of the Court.

Princess Augusta squeezed the hoop of her wide skirt to fit, filling the tube with giggles as she and her companions, including Emmeline and Fanny, entered the cool darkness. A troop of gentlemen followed, while some of the more delicate ladies insisted on remaining under the safety of their parasols in the sun. Caroline watched with amusement as the merry company marched through. Then she felt a hand at her elbow.

'*Mademoiselle*,' Lalande greeted her as if he hadn't been gone a day. 'Your party is a great success.'

Caroline could not stop a smile from dancing upon her lips. This time, there was no darkness to hide her happiness, or to hide Lalande's own eager look. She suddenly felt she was home – an odd realisation, for she *was* at home. But his presence calmed her: Lalande, there in a well-cut day suit, holding a posy of flowers. There was great commotion all around, yet she felt as if a lens had encircled just the two of them, cutting out everything else. She was hardly aware of how fully she could ignore all other people and conversation when he stood before her. The intimacy was immediate and complete.

'I brought…*un bouquet*,' Lalande said, suddenly more shy than flirtatious. Caroline hesitated. She feared she might say, or do, something to cause gossip.

'*C'est bon?*' A flicker of worry crossed Lalande's face. 'I hope it is not inappropriate.'

'Goodness, no!' Caroline said, taking up the posy and curtseying lightly. 'It's most welcome. *Merci, Monsieur*,' she murmured. She did not wish to be so formal, but could think of nothing better to do. This was not her rooftop, with the telescope, at night, nor was it the private comfort of her parlour – though she wished that it were. She found herself wishing the entire party and even William far, far away.

'Erik, bring these in to your mother, to place in water,' Caroline instructed, calling over the boy, who was helping to fill and clear plates and glasses. 'They're beautiful,' she said, smiling again at Lalande. 'Thank you.' She had never been given a posy, and later, alone, she would bury her nose in their delicate scent, feeling the silky petals brush her eyelids.

'Shall we walk, Miss Herschel?' Lalande asked, offering his arm. The light in his blue eyes was not dimmed, but dampened, and she welcomed the restraint blanketing his eagerness, like a fire that was banked for the night. When he turned the full fervour of his gaze on her, she felt desperately unsettled. She accepted his arm, and they began to stroll around the garden.

A second wave of guests prepared to make their journey through the forty-foot's tube. The King readied himself to go first. Without his wig, which he'd abandoned for his trip to the countryside, his short-cropped hair glistened with sweat. He chuckled at the Archbishop of Canterbury, who stood beside him grumbling. Caroline suppressed a giggle.

'I can't fit into the blasted thing with my hat,' the Archbishop complained.

The King snorted. 'Leave the Mitre, Sir,' he announced, holding out his hand. 'Come, My Lord Bishop, I will show you the way to Heaven!'

The tube filled with laughter as the frowning Bishop tugged off his tall mitre to follow the King's beckoning hand. Comments and jokes floated through the garden as the procession shuffled through and spilled, blinking, into the sunlight.

Caroline spotted William emerging from the parlour. He held his long-neglected violin in one hand, an oboe in the other. Rounding up Watson and a few footstools, he set up at one end of the now-clear tube.

'An acoustical experiment!' someone exclaimed, as they struck up a song. Caroline was pleased she'd kept the instruments in tune.

'*Magnifique*,' Lalande said, patting Caroline's hand, which was tucked into his arm.

Caroline shook her head with a laugh, ever amazed at her brother's ingenuity. He knew what he was doing, just as he had gained his post at the Octagon in Bath by placing lead weights on certain keys of the organ to produce an impossibly sonorous, four-handed sound. The gentlemen assessing musicians for the post had been astounded by William's virtuosity and hired him at once.

The tube hummed to life as notes filled the air. Caroline and Lalande watched as guests began to dance. Caroline found her throat tightening with emotion. To be playing music, in a giant telescope tube – only dear William would imagine making this instrument of the stars into an instrument of song. Notes carried across the garden, the sun shone warm, and the guests fairly sparkled with pleasure.

The party continued throughout the afternoon, into the warm evening. Chairs, picnic rugs, and chaise lounges were laid out, and Caroline brought down her reflector in order to show the Queen just how she swept the garden. Fanny was also interested in learning how the sweeps worked.

'Would Miss Beckedorff like to see the telescope, Miss Burney?' Caroline asked, careful to use formal names in front of formal company. The Queen glanced at Fanny and smiled.

'Excuse me, I shall find my husband,' the Queen said. 'Thank you for the lesson, Miss Herschel. I am enlightened.'

'Of course, Madame,' Caroline said, curtseying low as the Queen took her leave.

'Miss Herschel,' Fanny said, tucking Caroline's arm into her own and directing them towards a quiet part of the garden. 'Caroline.'

'Yes?' Caroline asked, mystified.

'Our dear Emmeline is quite enchanted by your brother, my friend,' Fanny whispered, smiling. 'I own I am surprised you did not see it before. She is trying to find an opportunity to speak with him this evening, to... provide some encouragement. He's been rather shy.'

Caroline paused, gathering her thoughts. Emmeline, smitten with William? She had not seen it at all. But she loved Emmeline, and the sweet woman would not make a bad match for her brother. There was, however, one problem.

'I am indeed surprised,' Caroline said slowly, working out her thoughts. 'While I would hate to see Emmeline disappointed, for I love her as a dear friend, I do wish I could warn her.'

'Warn her?' Fanny said, frowning.

'Well...my brother has no intention to marry,' Caroline said. 'He is wedded to his work. I would rather spare our friend any disappointment. Do you see?'

Fanny looked across the garden and Caroline followed her gaze. The space was dotted with candles, placed here and there in jam jars along the tables and throughout the garden. Some candles hung in lanterns on shepherd's hooks stuck into the grass, suspending the lights at various heights, some as tall as a man, some on the ground. As dusk gave way to night, the tiny brilliances gave the effect that the party floated on their chaises and blankets in a warm, starlit sky.

In one candlelit part of the garden, William sat, in conversation with Emmeline Beckedorff. She leaned close and laughed with him, but his attention did not seem wholly focused on her. They were not alone – another couple sat with them. Caroline recognised the pair as Mr and Mrs Pitt, neighbours to Observatory House. Mr Pitt was much older than his wife, and not in the best of health. Caroline was pleased to see he felt well enough to attend the party, though she noted he was wrapped in more than one blanket, and the night wasn't cold in the least. William leaned in to say something, and this time Mary Pitt let out a peal of laughter.

'You see, Fanny?' Caroline said, pulling off her bonnet, unneeded in the dusk. 'William doesn't bestow particular favour on her.'

Fanny gave her a long look that Caroline couldn't read in the dark.

'You are right, my dear,' Fanny said quietly. 'His favour is not focused on her.' She hesitated. 'Sometimes,' she added gently, 'we spend all our lives looking, yet we fail to see things right before our eyes. Perhaps there is danger in looking too far afield.'

Caroline frowned. She was about to ask Fanny the meaning of her cryptic statement when Lalande appeared with two glasses to hand.

'May I interest you in a drink, *mademoiselles*?' he asked with a slight bow of the head. Fanny pressed Caroline's hand.

'I'm going to collect my friend,' she said with a light laugh, 'and drag her into a game of whist. But thank you, *monsieur*.' She turned, gave Caroline a kiss on the cheek, and swept off towards Emmeline, calling, '*au revoir*'.

'Well,' Lalande said, holding out a glass to Caroline. 'A drink for me, then, I suppose. Let us toast to your comet!'

Caroline raised her glass and took a sip of wine. It was the first mention anyone had made of her comet that night. If she wanted anyone to mention it, it was Lalande.

'Here's to many more discoveries,' Lalande said, leading Caroline to a pair of chairs near the hollyhocks.

Caroline took another sip of wine, her nerves tingling. There was so much she wished to say, about comets, discoveries, Messier…

'I have missed our conversations,' Lalande said quietly, and Caroline resisted the urge to take up his hand.

'As have I,' she answered, her voice tight. Why, her mind shouted, could they not act in public as they did in private? They were merely friends. And if there was affection – would that be wrong? She noticed not a few of the courtiers had absconded to darker corners of the garden. Giggles and whispers skipped across the lawn.

'*Carolina,*' Lalande said, his accent intensifying. He took up her hand; her glass fell to the ground. Their knees almost touched in the darkness. She felt everything dropping away. His blue eyes and bald head shone in the candlelight. Her mind could not even form the word *kiss*. Lalande's face was inches from hers. She caught the scent of coffee and a touch of garlic.

'The Paris Observatory would celebrate a Lady Astronomer as she should be celebrated,' Lalande said breathlessly. 'Just imagine it – you and I, working together, you discovering comets, your name beside Messier and Lalande—'

Caroline pulled back, the words jolting her as if she'd fallen from the rickety twenty-foot.

'What?' she stammered, 'What are you proposing?'

The starlit garden seemed to tilt on its axis.

'Paris! Come to France with me,' Lalande urged, his hand tight around hers. 'Leave your brother behind and receive the attention you deserve. I will help with all the arrangements.'

'*Leave your brother behind…*'

Horrified, Caroline pulled from his grasp, stumbling from the chair. She glared at him.

'I thought…I *thought* you understood the import of my brother's work,' Caroline said in dismay, her hand gripping her worry-bead so hard it hurt. 'I thought you knew how important his work was to me. I have agreed to be William's assistant, no one else's.' Her voice dropped to a whisper and she glanced over her shoulder before locking her gaze with his once more. 'And how *dare you* ask me to leave my work for the King and Queen this very night?'

Lalande stood, taking her hands. He was much taller than she, and she felt insignificant beside him. She felt he could envelop her, and the thought was both tempting and terrifying. She could lose herself with him; she could be lost with him.

'Of course I understand how important it is, *Carolina*. As important as I find my own work. This is why you should come, and receive what is due to you. Here, you are diminished in the glory of your brother's glow. A smaller star, orbiting a greater one, just like William's doubles. Set out with me, and you shall be the greater.'

Caroline struggled against the draw of Lalande's passionate words. Some of what he said rang true, she could admit. But not all of it would seem as magical as it did that night, and she could admit that as well.

'I will not leave my role beside my brother to take up a role beside you,' she said, gently but firmly. 'I will not leave one star to pale beside another.'

'*Mademoiselle, je t'adore*,' Lalande whispered, cupping her face in his hands. 'You will never pale.'

If he would only kiss her, perhaps then she would know how to choose. She had never been kissed. Lalande ran his thumb over her lips. She shuddered and closed her eyes. Then his hand fell away.

'You break my heart, *mademoiselle*,' Lalande said. 'I hope you do not come to regret this choice.'

When she opened her eyes, he was gone.

Chapter 15

With the party a success, the solstice well behind them, and the nights shortening, William resumed charting double stars with the twenty-foot. Now that the garden party was done, the forty-foot tube and mirror could be mounted, but they had to arrange no fewer than ten men and six horses for the task.

Her brother would never realise something was wrong unless he fell eight metres from a rickety post, or she left a fillet of flesh behind on a hook. Caroline tried not to resent the fact that he acted the same as he always had. To all appearances, there was no reason for the rhythm of their lives to be any different, but she felt as if the poles of her world had swapped north and south.

She could do nothing without thinking of Lalande: his warm hand holding hers; the depths of emotion in his eyes. If Fanny or Emmeline had been so smitten, Caroline would have brought out the smelling salts. She wanted someone to give her a good shake and tell her she must pull herself together. But still she missed him. In her mind, each letter that arrived was from Paris; each footstep in the garden was his. But he did not appear, and no letters came.

Finally, when William pointed out not one but two errors in her calculations from a night's work, she resolved to take action. The next time William was called to the Castle, she went with him. Windsor was as sumptuous as she remembered, but the usual gaiety of the company was dampened. Scanning the crowds for one bald, tall Frenchman, Caroline also sought her friends to discover the reason for the gloomy atmosphere.

'Rumour has it the King is ill,' Fanny said mournfully as they settled into a corner sofa. 'The poor Queen is all nerves. We don't know what is wrong, but he had a fit of some kind two days ago and has spoken to no one since.'

'Another reason to be melancholy,' Emmeline said with a sigh, resting her chin on her hand. Her eyes filled with tears.

'My dear, it will be alright,' Fanny said, patting Emmeline's hand. 'It's hard for her to see you,' she said to Caroline. 'Emmeline is heartsick over William.'

'I *am* sorry,' Caroline said, reaching for her worry-bead. 'If only I had known, Emmeline, I would have warned you – I didn't know…' she hesitated. 'I don't understand the secrets of love. I only feel we Herschels are poor at playing the game.'

Emmeline nodded and wiped her tears away. 'It will not kill me, that much I'm sure of,' she said. She sighed again.

'It will not indeed,' Fanny said firmly. 'But for the secrets of love, Caroline, I think you know more than you admit. One guest in particular enjoyed the garden party, did he not? Am I right to venture that the French astronomer admires our comet-seeker?'

As her friends looked at her quizzically, Caroline's spirits sank even lower. 'But that's why I've come to Windsor,' she blurted, 'I wished awfully to see Lalande, but he isn't here. Is he? I've seen neither hide nor hair of him.'

'My dear, did you arrange to meet?' Fanny asked, leaning forward.

'No, nothing of the sort,' Caroline said. 'I only wish to see him. We've arranged nothing. But at the garden party, well – he made a proposal –'

'He *proposed*?' Emmeline wailed. 'Oh, it's not *fair*! Now I feel more alone than ever!'

'No!' Caroline broke in. 'He made a proposal. That I should come to Paris – to work in the Observatory. With him.' Even as she spoke the words, she could hear how unlikely they sounded. Her friends stared.

'He has made no offer of marriage?' Fanny said.

Caroline shook her head.

'Has he kissed you, professed his love in any way?' Emmeline asked. Again, Caroline responded in the negative.

'But it has seemed – he has come close. He has said he adores me, and…oh!' she clapped her hands into her lap in frustration. 'But I refused him. I refused it all. And now I don't know whether I shall ever see him again, and I can think of nothing else. I can hardly eat or sleep!'

'My dear girl,' Fanny said, now patting Caroline's hand, and offering a kerchief for her tears, 'you're in love.'

Caroline sniffed into the kerchief.

'Would you go, if he made a proper offer?' Fanny asked.

'I don't know,' Caroline moaned. 'I don't think I could leave William.'

Emmeline frowned into her glass of dessert wine.

'I can think of nothing more exciting, or romantic, than eloping with a Frenchman,' Fanny sighed. 'Just think – Paris!'

'Moving from Hanover to England, leaving singing for astronomy – all were excitement enough,' Caroline said.

'But what of romance?' Emmeline whispered. Her frowned deepened, and she shot a glance across the room to an oblivious William, who stood talking with Joseph Banks. 'Or has your family no feelings at all on the subject?'

'Emmeline!' Fanny admonished.

She looked chastened. 'I'm sorry, Caroline,' she murmured. 'But it's quite dismal to be in love and not feel it returned. Once you're certain of what you have, do not waste it.'

Chapter 16

The rest of the summer and burnished autumn were taken up with viewing. When William was at home, Caroline was by his side, taking notes. When he was at Court, she stood on her roof and swept. Her friend's words turned over and over in her mind, and rather than becoming more certain about her feelings, she grew less sure.

She loved Lalande, and together, they shared a love of astronomy. But was this any different from what she had with William? She was not about to leave her role as her brother's assistant to become someone else's. If Lalande had given any hint of marriage, she might feel differently, but it had not been mentioned.

Through the confusion of her feelings, Caroline resolved to lose herself in the skies. The indifferent emptiness of the heavens, and the order of charting stars on paper, proved a comforting contrast to the mess of emotions. The Star Catalogue fulfilled her need for distraction.

Compiled by the first Astronomer Royal, John Flamsteed, The Star Catalogue marked the location of nearly three thousand stars in the northern sky. Though rightfully celebrated as the most accurate work of its day, Caroline had discovered numerous errors: many of the 'fixed' stars were not fixed at the coordinates Flamsteed had listed. Each star's set of coordinates needed checking, both on paper and in the sky.

They'd only realised this after William encountered difficulty locating some of the stars in the Catalogue during his sweeps. He thought they had burnt out, or spun out of orbit. William attributed inconsistencies with the lustre of the real stars compared to the lustre noted by Flamsteed to a change in the burning power of the star itself. It had taken Caroline to point out that perhaps Flamsteed the man had been fallible, rather than the heavens being so changeable. After some debate, William agreed. He then proposed that she amend the Catalogue. It offered plenty to occupy her in the interstices between assisting him and sweeping for comets. And though William did not know it, the work saved her from indulging in heartsickness when rain fell, or the sky was overcast.

Due to the imminently useful nature of such a tedious project, the Royal Society offered to pay for publication of Caroline's corrections, most notably the omitted stars. She had begun the project only at William's encouragement, but as she worked on into the depths of autumn, she began to feel that each star deserved to be accounted for. Each burned with its own light; each held its own place in the firmament. Each was one point in an asterism or constellation of greater or lesser import, and Caroline did her best to ensure no star was overlooked.

It became a kind of obsession: she mustn't miss out any star. Each had shone over an unthinkable amount of time and space. That one should go unnoticed after the light had travelled for thousands of years, as William claimed, struck Caroline as an awful tragedy. The star may have died out long before she was born, long before the Greeks began naming the first planets. The fossil light, falling in faint rays, through the tubes of William's telescopes, finally reaching her eye, absolutely had to be marked in the Catalogue.

By the end of September, Caroline had the courage to pick up her pen and write to Lalande. She resumed the warm but distanced tone of their earlier missives, telling him all about her work with William, with sweeping, and with the Catalogue. She enquired after his health, and his work.

'It flatters my vanity not a little,' she wrote, 'that my corrections have been taken up for publication by the Royal Society.'

The night after posting the letter, Caroline spotted another comet. The wave of letters and enthusiasm that followed buoyed her mood until she had a reply from Paris. In the same cordial tone, Lalande shared tidings of his work. He had also heard of her second comet, and congratulated her.

'Was there ever a woman without vanity?' he wrote, and she could almost hear the teasing tones of his voice. 'Or a man either?'

Before penning her reply, she looked across the room to William, who was fastidiously adding stars to his three-dimensional drawing.

'There is this difference,' she wrote, 'among gentlemen, the commodity is generally called *ambition*.'

'It's very like a ship, don't you think?' Mary Pitt murmured, her pretty brow furrowed in consideration.

'It rather is, ma'am, with its struts and spars and ladders,' William replied. 'A good description to bring back to your husband, to help him envision it.'

'I'm sorry he isn't well enough to venture out and see it complete,' Mary said, casting her eyes to the ground.

'As are we,' William answered gently. 'It's good of you to come, to view it in his stead.'

'Oh,' Mary said, her round face breaking into a smile, 'it is not entirely out of charity, Mr Herschel – I too wished to see the telescope.'

William chuckled.

Caroline watched the exchange with a frown. This charity towards their neighbours was an unexpected development. She entirely supported William's kindness towards the Pitts – Mary must be suffering as her husband wasted away under the grip of illness. But it pained Caroline to watch William's forced jollity towards Mary, when she knew he was in fact full of discontent over the forty-foot.

'The mirror tarnishes so rapidly I can hardly see a thing!' This was William's first complaint over the colossal telescope. Then, 'the blasted lens condenses at any vapour – even my breath!'

His criticisms paused when he discovered, using the forty-foot, a tiny moon orbiting Saturn. He christened it Mimas, son of the goddess Gaia. Ever since the astronomical community had insisted on re-naming his planet, William had chosen Greek names for his discoveries. Letters from Windsor, Paris, and the Royal Society arrived at Obs House; replies travelled back thanks to Caroline's assisting pen. But this moon was the only thing of import William found with the giant telescope, and he ultimately considered it a failure.

Now, standing before the forty-foot, the garden leaves bronzed by the cool touch of late autumn, Caroline had to watch as William once again pretended enthusiasm for the scope. It had indeed been added to the Ordinance Survey map, and visitors stopped by day and night to see it. Few understood how ineffective it was as an instrument. He'd overreached; William said so himself. The telescope loomed. Had the old trees been left standing, it would have been taller than them all, a great eye looking out to the heavens.

'…once again, thank you for showing me,' Mary Pitt was saying. Caroline smiled and offered the lady a small curtsey.

'You must come for supper someday soon – both of you,' Mary added. 'My husband would like that. A little company cheers him.'

'Of course, we'd be delighted,' William said, 'and you must let us know if there's anything at all we can do…' he continued, leading Mary down the walk.

Caroline watched them for a moment, looked up once more at the great telescope, and absently grasped her worry-bead before retreating to the house. Flamsteed's Catalogue beckoned.

'Discovering a third and then a fourth comet, Miss Herschel, why, this is unprecedented, is it not?' John Pitt cleared his throat and smiled weakly from across his soup.

The poor man hardly seemed to eat. Caroline rested her fork on her plate, feeling strange enjoying the slices of honeyed pork that Mary had prepared for the rest of them.

'Indeed,' William answered warmly, 'even Messier has written to congratulate her.'

'And who, dare I ask, is Messier?' Mary asked, her pink cheeks a striking contrast to her husband's papery countenance. She sat close by his side, helping him to eat.

'A French astronomer,' William replied, once more answering before Caroline was able to gather her thoughts. 'The best. He's well known for his own discoveries of comets.'

Caroline raised an eyebrow and plucked up her fork.

'There is more than one talented French astronomer,' she said. The dull ache of missing Lalande had almost become a comfort. Her eyes met the gaze of John Pitt across the table, but he only looked tired, not sympathetic.

'There are at least two talented English ones,' Mary said with a smile, raising her glass. 'To your discoveries, Miss Herschel – congratulations.'

'Thank you,' Caroline murmured.

Caroline reckoned it must be the growing aches in William's bones that encouraged him to visit their neighbours more often than sweep the skies on cold

106

nights. She was not best pleased at his visits to John and Mary Pitt at Upton.

'It's an uncommonly *cozy* situation, the three of you,' she said one afternoon as William prepared for supper, once again at Upton. 'Surely you take time away from Mrs Pitt's care of her husband?'

He'd scoffed.

'Not at all, Lina, I go because John himself asks it of me. Mrs Pitt says he likes the company, and I'm happy to oblige such a kind old man.' He peered into the mirror hanging beside the long-case clock and adjusted his cravat.

'I only think it best not to become too closely involved with the affairs of others,' Caroline said. 'Besides, William, we're missing time at the telescopes.'

'All the more opportunity for you to discover your comets,' William said, kissing her on the forehead before he left.

She had indeed discovered more comets. After news of the fourth had spread, the invitation to Upton was extended to include her. She did not know whether William had prompted this. Nonetheless, she resolved to be sociable, and attend.

Now she sat, curled on a settle by the fire, John Pitt dozing in an armchair. She watched the slow rise and fall of his chest: at times, there was such a long pause between breaths that it seemed he had already passed on to the next world. A low laugh drew her eye to the card-table by the window, where William and Mary sat. Mary's eyes sparkled in the candlelight, and Caroline felt a flash of pity for the lady, who was, no doubt, soon to be a widow. But she admitted that William was right, and if John enjoyed their company, it seemed to do Mary good, too. Caroline only hoped William didn't take much more time from their work. Gazing at the flickering firelight, she sighed. It would have been a good night for comet sweeping.

When Caroline learned of John Pitt's death less than a month later, her sympathy for Mary Pitt was distracted by a letter from Paris. Lalande would return to Windsor at Christmastide. She resolved to complete her corrections of Flamsteed's Catalogue of Stars in time for Lalande's visit. If he was to attend Court that winter, so would she.

The autumn was full of work, which helped ease the wait for Lalande. By night, she assisted William at his twenty-foot, which had proven far more useful than the forty-foot. He had taken to surveying nebulae as well as double stars. These were extraordinarily distant, cloud-like objects: some bright, some faint, some in clusters. On her own sweeps, Caroline began to find nebulae as well as comets, adding to William's list. She learned to distinguish the fuzzy streak of a comet from the blurry amorphous shape of a nebula, sketching them as she saw them.

Over breakfast, William would ponder with her over just what they were seeing. Were new stars coming into being in these swirling centres of light and energy? Was the very existence of the cosmos evident in its furthest reaches? It was a job for those who thrived on questions rather than answers, and they asked many.

Late mornings were for letter writing, with afternoons devoted to checks on the Star Catalogue. Evenings were for cooking and cleaning, for eating supper, and for sewing and mending, though Hannah helped ease the burden of everyday housework.

The days moved on as the nights lengthened, giving Caroline time to sweep in the small hours before sunrise. Though the anticipation of seeing Lalande again grew with each passing day, there was still the Catalogue to finish. Caroline lost herself in work.

On the first snowfall of the year, when the Cottage, telescopes, house and grounds glittered under a dusting of silvery white, she discovered another comet. Joseph Banks and Nevil Maskelyne paid a visit, and Caroline relished the chance to clear the table of astronomical charts and lay a proper dinner for them. She and William had never been so comfortably ensconced in astronomical endeavours. Without obligations to the Royals due to the cold weather, they were able to enjoy their work, and the wisdom of learned friends.

Thus Caroline was all the more surprised when William, after congratulating her on her successful dinner with their guests, suggested inviting Mary Pitt to dine the following week.

'But that is surely too snug a situation for a recently-widowed woman,' Caroline protested. The lady was sweet, yes, but why bring someone into the house that could not contribute to or properly enjoy philosophical work? 'She and I are not the best of friends, William, kind as she may be, and John Pitt, rest his soul, has barely been dead three months.'

'Be kind, Lina,' William said, a note of warning in his voice. 'Mrs Pitt is our friend. Surely it will give her some relief to leave the house, with its painful memories, and enjoy the company of neighbours. Besides,' he said with pleasure, setting aside his papers, 'she's demonstrated a real interest in the telescopes. And she can only see those here at Obs House.'

Caroline frowned, jabbing a few stitches through the lace of a shirt cuff. 'If you see fit, Brother, but do have a care,' she said. 'After all, the neighbours are sure to talk.'

William barked out a laugh. 'If you mean that old crow Mrs Papendiek, let her. She dreams up enough gossip as it is.'

Mary Pitt demonstrated only the most basic understanding of the telescopes. It was a struggle to see what the widow enjoyed in William's musings on ecliptics and nebulae. Though she knew her brooding silence wasn't particularly welcoming towards their guest, Caroline ignored the pleading glances William directed across the table as they ate.

For her part, Mary Pitt appeared unchanged by her husband's death. She was still rosy-cheeked and soft-spoken. The clink of cutlery was broken only by William's quiet comments as he worked to uphold the conversation. When the talk turned to Mary's estate and some assistance he might be regarding financial papers, Caroline wished she were anywhere else. She toyed with her worry-bead with one hand as she pushed potatoes around her plate with her fork.

'Sister?'

'Pardon me,' Caroline said, forcing a smile. 'I was daydreaming.'

'How goes your sweeping, Miss Herschel?' Mary asked, obviously repeating the question.

'Fine, fine, thank you,' Caroline said, thinking that it was not *going* at all, because she had to sit at the table and host this dinner. Well, if the lady wanted astronomical talk, she should have it. Why must they change the usual theme of their conversation, when they were at a place known as Observatory House?

'I've been carrying out corrections on Flamsteed's Star Catalogue these past months,' Caroline continued, 'and working on calculations converting sidereal time into solar time,' she spoke more rapidly as she gained momentum, 'which of course depends on the precession of equinoxes; the orthogonal second axis of the Earth's rotation –'

'Lina, please,' William broke in, smiling tightly from across the table.

Mary looked bewildered. 'That…that sounds impressive, Miss Herschel,' she murmured.

Caroline took a sip of wine.

'Forgive me, Mrs Pitt,' she said, lowering her glass. 'I shall speak more simply. I didn't intend to overwhelm you with mathematics. Our work goes well: I've recently discovered another comet.'

Mary broke into a smile, and William nodded in relief.

Later, Caroline relented, carrying her sweeper down from the roof of the Cottage to show Mary how it worked.

'I'm afraid I can't make out a thing,' Mary said, peering through the scope.

'That's not uncommon,' Caroline said, and this time her smile was genuine. 'It takes a great deal of practice.'

Chapter 17

'I'll be *damned*!' William growled, slamming a letter onto the dining table. Caroline cringed, pushing aside the Star Catalogue.

'He doesn't understand, even after all this time, he does *not* understand – ' William fretted, pouring over the letter, stabbing at it with his finger.

Caroline waited for the storm of his mood to calm so he would explain.

'His *Highness*,' William said through his teeth, 'listened to Banks's petition regarding my running costs. You know how much we need for the upkeep of the scopes. Apparently the King *stormed* at Banks – raged at him.' He shook his head, finger running over the letter again. So, this was news from Banks; and it sounded bad indeed.

'The King agreed to everything,' William went on, 'but he said he expected quicker results and would provide not a farthing more, after this, towards our aid. *Blast*. If the man wasn't going mad, we'd know better what to expect.'

He threw himself into a dining chair and began to scribble a reply.

Caroline pressed her hands to her eyes. William's writing was a scrawl at the best of times; in this mood, it would be illegible. She wished he would dictate to her, so she could write it in a fair hand and make Banks's reading of it less traumatising than whatever critical words it contained.

'Wait, Brother,' Caroline said gently, the meaning of his words coming clear. 'The King agreed to everything? ...*Everything*? But surely this is a cause for celebration, even if the meeting itself was not a great success. Our aims are met!' As she spoke, her words became warmer, and William paused.

'William – this means, that I – ?'

'Yes, Lina,' he said, twirling the quill in his hand, spattering ink across the page. 'The Queen has granted you a salary as my assistant, for all of your accomplishments.' He broke into a smile, shaking his head. 'I'm sorry; the King's mood seems to be affecting my own. You know I could not do this without you. Congratulations.'

'Oh, William!' Caroline cried, throwing her arms around him. She would have an annual income. She'd finally be able to provide for herself.

It was the aim she had reached for since she was small. Frau Herschel had barred fancy needlework to ensure Caroline would never become a seamstress; had barred dancing and languages to ensure she would never become a governess; had barred music to ensure she would never become a performer. Miss Carsten had taught her needlework; Mrs Colebrook had taught her dancing; William had taught her music.

And Frau Herschel would never have reckoned on *astronomy*, which William had taught her as well. It was the astronomy that was finally allowing her to earn her keep. She'd fretted over her dependence since she was a girl, stuck as a maid in Hanover; since Bath, when she regretted declining the offer to sing at Birmingham. Since the garden party, when she rejected Lalande's offer to go to Paris. Now, she was being recognised for the work she carried out by William's side, with an income from no less a person than the Queen of England.

William patted her on the shoulder and nodded, the mix of frustration and joy flitting across his face like clouds across the skies of Holland.

'What troubles you, Brother?' Caroline asked. 'The King's moods? They think he is very ill, you know; it isn't due to Banks, or us.'

'No, it isn't that, Lina,' William said. 'It is his wording, his approach. To expect *results* – why, this is no planet-producing workshop! We are explorers, adventurers, casting out into the unknown. We've compiled hundreds of nebulae and a pocket-full of comets. Your work on the Flamsteed Catalogue will be invaluable to astronomers the world over. I only…' his voice faded and he ran his hands through his hair. The pen rested on his letter to Banks, ink dripping into a blotch, spreading across the page. She would have to write it for him anyhow.

'All will be well, Brother,' Caroline said quietly, squeezing his shoulder.

She knew what he could not bring himself to say. The forty-foot had failed, and the majority of work they carried out was, for the most part, far from the stuff of legend. Just as she was the double to William's star, his planet outshone him. The great discovery that had sparked his career and brought him the attention of the King was also the success he could never best. If William's star had shone brightest those years ago in Bath, now there was nothing for it but to burn out.

Chapter 18

Windsor Castle was specially bedecked for the Christmas season. They approached via the Long Walk in a carriage sent to Observatory House expressly to fetch them. The King sending a carriage seemed to prove that he bore them no ill will. As they neared the Castle, they rattled past hundreds of pairs of elm trees framing the drive, and Caroline felt a fleeting nostalgia for the elms William had cut down. They passed merry-makers building shapes in the snow, and more bawdily dressed figures, bundled in cheap velvets, who flashed pale wrists and ankles to entice wayward gentlemen. Caroline peered out of the carriage window, her cloak close around her shoulders, marveling at the silver-grey bulk of Windsor dusted with the spectacle of snow. Enormous swathes of evergreen boughs had been plaited, and hung from the Castle windows.

They were shown into the State Reception Room, where candlelight bounced from chandeliers, and mirrors winked the length of the hall. A blaze roared in the marble fireplace, easily taller than Caroline herself. People mingled, some playing cards, others perched on sofas or warming themselves by the fire, enjoying glasses of wine.

Though Caroline refused to involve herself in gossip, she could not help but overhear whispers of the King's indisposition, and the Prince pressing for Regency. The Queen, when Caroline curtsied before her, was kind as ever, but her interest in sweeping the garden had faded in light of more pressing matters. Caroline withdrew from the Queen after a brief audience, feeling sympathetic for the lady. Without appearing to look too eager, she searched the room for Lalande, but spotted a different familiar face.

'Miss Burney!' Caroline greeted her friend with delight. 'It has been an age since we last met.'

Her friend greeted her with a kiss on each cheek, and blushed. 'Indeed it has, my dear Miss Herschel. But I am called Madame D'Arblay now, for I've been married,' Fanny said, fluttering a fan in front of her mouth to hide a wide smile. 'Forgive me for not staying in touch as I should; my husband and I have been caught up in the troubles in France.'

So, Fanny had wed! Caroline congratulated her friend, recalling the heavy-hearted sigh Fanny had given when they last spoke: *'I can think of nothing more exciting, or romantic, than eloping with a Frenchman,'* – And she had done just that. Caroline realised that even back then, her friend might have been speaking of a particular Frenchman of her own affections, but Caroline had been too distracted with Lalande to notice.

'What of the Emperor Bonaparte, Madame D'Arblay?' William asked, appearing at Caroline's side. He had been ensconced in conversation elsewhere, but Caroline was grateful for his input on world affairs, which she knew little about.

Snapping her fan shut, Fanny glared. 'Indeed, France becomes treacherous, and my husband and I are likely to remain in London for the time,' she said. 'Though it has been somewhat easier to sail since Admiral Nelson, bless the man, has been engaged on our side.'

How could one part of the world be at war, Caroline wondered, while her small sphere at Observatory House remained entirely untouched? The Continent, once home, felt like a separate planet. The only effect the siblings had felt was a small shock in the form of a letter announcing Jacob's death in battle. Caroline had barely mourned him; her youth in Hanover felt like a lifetime away.

'Ah, Nelson!' William said, pressing his hand to his breast. 'Now, tell me, Madame…'

His voice faded as Caroline's sweeps of the room finally fixed on the person she sought. Lalande stood amongst a group of men, and he too seemed to search the crowd. The letters, the months of waiting, the refusal of his offer, and how awfully she missed the sound of his voice – she could feel the longing in everything, all at once. She wished to pretend she had not seen him, so he would approach first. She murmured a pardon and moved slowly across the room towards him, the surrounding conversations dulling into a hum.

Spotting her, Lalande made his excuses and hastened over. Ever composed, he offered his arm, and guided her out onto a terrace. Caroline no longer cared who saw, or if people talked. A servant offered them cloaks as they made their way out of a set of French doors, and Lalande twirled the thick black velvet over Caroline's shoulders. It was far too long for her, and she gathered it up, the fox-fur lining spreading warmth into her hands. She laughed.

'We seem ready to do battle with a snow monster,' she said. Lalande's cloak matched hers; the fur enhanced the icy blue of his eyes. They walked across the terrace, Lalande careful not to let Caroline slip on the icy stones. She could just make out the eye of the forty-foot in the evening darkness in the forest below Windsor, and pointed it out. Buried in the cloak, she pushed back the sleeve and made sure he saw where she gestured.

'Oh, I have missed you,' Lalande said, gathering her hands in his. 'And your 'Obs House', and your comets. And – this,' he said, pressing her hands. 'There is so much to share, Miss Herschel.'

'Your book,' Caroline said, unsure of what to say. 'Is it published?'

Lalande nodded.

'I have wished you were here,' Caroline murmured, wanting to explain how she'd longed for his company. 'I've wanted to tell you of each discovery, each mistake. The Star Catalogue – everything.'

Lalande nodded again, his eyes peering into hers so keenly she had to look away.

'Miss Herschel – *Carolina*,' he said, and she met his gaze. 'I am sorry for the way I left the garden party. It was cruel of me. I was so disappointed, you see…'

'Hush,' Caroline said, 'I understand.'

'I wanted…' Lalande said, leaning close, 'not to speak, but to *act*. May I?'

Caroline nodded, her throat tight. The stars, the frost, the crowd in the State Room – all flew out of her head.

Gathering her into his arms with the thick folds of velvet, Lalande kissed her. It was the sweetest, gentlest thing, as if she was made of spun glass, and might shatter into a thousand fragments. She felt as if she might do just that: she wanted to break apart, to weep with joy at his tenderness. Despite her refusal, all was not lost.

'Surely you have reconsidered?' Lalande whispered, holding her close. His arms enveloped her and she felt more safe, more cared for, than she had ever known. She wanted nothing more than to accept, to give herself up to this, no matter the consequences for herself, her work, or William.

She hesitated, and Lalande sighed, brushing a kiss just above her eyes.

'You know the offer, *Carolina*: Paris, the Observatory. Work with me in France.'

This was not marriage.

'Oh,' Caroline gave a small sigh, sinking into his arms. 'I have missed you.'

'Then do not allow us to miss each other like this ever again,' Lalande murmured. 'We do not have to be separated this way.'

'Would you leave Paris?' she asked.

Lalande gave her a bewildered look. 'Leave Paris? Permanently? *Pourquoi*? My work, my home, is there.'

Caroline smiled wryly. '*Précicément*,' she said, 'as mine is here.'

'But it could be in Paris,' Lalande said, turning her chin to him and smiling. His charm was irresistible. Almost.

'I am William's assistant,' Caroline argued, her heart feeling split in two. 'My work is indispensable to him.'

Lalande kissed her again.

'I love you,' he murmured. 'But it is not enough.'

'And I love you,' Caroline choked, her eyes filling with prisms of tears. The candlelight from sconces burning on either side of the French doors blurred; they looked like comets.

'But I cannot make you choose,' Lalande said, gently grasping her shoulders. 'At least, not choose the answer I want. You love your brother, and your devotion to him is too strong – it is admirable,' he said, cutting off Caroline's protests, 'I admit it is admirable. But you do not know how ardently I wish that your devotion were for *me*, and no other. How I wish to be the one viewing the stars by your side at night, working out calculations with you in the morning, and dining with you in the evening. I wish – ' here Lalande's voice faltered, and his accent thickened, 'I wish you had chosen *me*, my love. For you cannot have us both.'

With a sob, Caroline threw her arms around him. He held her as she wept. He was right. She had devoted her life to William, and though it broke her heart, she would not waver from her decision.

*

The frosty night endeavoured to drive them indoors, but the cloaks kept off the chill, and Caroline would have been pleased to freeze in Lalande's arms. It was Miss Beckedorff who broke the spell, venturing onto the terrace in search of Caroline.

'Miss Herschel?' came the tentative whisper. Caroline and Lalande stepped briskly apart.

'I'm here, Miss Beckedorff,' Caroline said.

'Madame D'Arblay, that is, Fanny,' Emmeline said, coming nearer, 'and I have been looking for you all evening. Will you come join us? We've missed your company all these months.' She paused. 'You must join us as well, Monsieur Lalande.'

'*Merci*, Miss,' Lalande answered from the folds of his cloak, 'but I shall be readying to leave in the morning, and must say my farewells.'

Caroline grasped the icy stone balustrade. The cold shot up her palms, making her wrists ache. Leaving, tomorrow?

'Very well,' Emmeline said, curtseying. 'Miss Herschel, we shall be near the fireplace in the Ballroom – will you find us there?'

'Yes,' Caroline managed to say, 'I'll join you shortly.'

'Tomorrow?' Caroline wailed after Emmeline left.

'I cannot stay,' Lalande said, 'it will kill me to see you, now that – ' he did not finish. 'Here,' he said, reaching for the small white rose decorating his button-hole. He slid a blade from his boot, cutting the flower free and offering it to Caroline. 'To remember me by.'

Trying to keep the trembling in her ribs from welling up into tears, Caroline tugged a lock of hair free from its pins, and tilted her head towards him. He drew the blade across the blonde curl, winding it around his fingers, and held it to his lips.

'You smell of winter, my love, and stardust,' he murmured.

She wanted to laugh, and to cry. 'If I was certain I would see you again, I should not let you say such frivolous things to me!' she wailed.

Lalande bowed his head. 'I will take my leave, and then, you must go to your friends,' he said. 'There will be less talk if we return separately, and good-byes are less painful if done quickly.'

Caroline nodded. This was more painful than the icy night the workmen lifted her from the hook in her leg. This time, the hook was in her heart, and there was no one to lift her free. With a final bow, Lalande gathered his cloak, and disappeared into the busy rooms of the Castle.

Biting her lip to keep from trembling, Caroline dug under the folds of the cloak. She pulled out the worry-bead, unscrewed it, and tossed the old, dark lock of William's hair over the balustrade. She kissed the rose before tucking it into the bead and returning the bead to her pocket. He would be in her thoughts, and this small gift would be with her, always.

Windsor had lost some of its shine in the time she'd spent on the terrace. Two hours at most had passed, and Caroline was again amazed at how time seemed to change when we was with Lalande; how they spun out of orbit into a world of their own. She made her way hazily to the Ballroom, where Emmeline and Fanny waited for her with a goblet of negus.

As the hot spiced wine flowed down her throat and into her belly, Caroline realised she had not frozen into marble as she'd wished. She had grown cold on the terrace – as usual, being with Lalande made her forget her senses. But as feeling returned to her thawing limbs, she regretted drinking the negus, for she *hurt*. If this was the meaning of heartache, it was miserable.

Emmeline squeezed Caroline's hand. 'I know, my dear,' she whispered. 'I know.'

Chapter 19

Nothing less than the discovery of another comet would satisfy her. With corrections on Flamsteed's Catalogue of Stars complete, and a date fixed for publication by the Royal Society, Caroline felt she must accomplish something more. As ever, she took notes for William when he swept with the twenty-foot on most clear nights, but the cold had begun to affect him, and they broke up the long winter evenings by inviting friends to dine. Guests varied from dear Dr Watson to Aubert, Banks, another visit from Alexander, and even an appearance from the widow Mary Pitt, who did not have far to travel.

Caroline welcomed any distraction, from roasting chickens, shoulders of mutton, and joints of pork, to practicing songs on the spinet. It had hardly been played since they moved from Bath, and the songs entertained their guests. She had little desire to sleep – sleep brought dreams best avoided. She spent the dark hours of early morning hunting the skies for comets.

It really was luck, Caroline told herself, sighting her seventh comet on an early spring night. Her corrections to the Star Catalogue had been published, to reviews of gratitude from astronomers in England and abroad. It was already proving extremely useful to researchers the world over: no surprise, for the Catalogue was a major reference for any stargazer, professional or amateur.

Nevil Maskelyne wrote from the Royal Observatory at Greenwich, sending his congratulations for the Catalogue, and inviting her to visit. He also confirmed her comet.

'We shall *get* this branch of astronomical business from the French,' the Astronomer Royal wrote gleefully, 'by *seeing* comets sooner and *observing* them later!'

Nevil and Sophia Maskelyne had invited Caroline to Greenwich numerous times throughout their long correspondence, but she hadn't ridden far on horseback since travelling from Hanover: after their carriage at Dover had overturned, they'd ridden into London. Since that journey, she'd been in Mrs Colebrook's carriage, and in carriages bringing her to Obs House or Windsor Castle. William used to ride his mare from Bath to London, willy-nilly, but Caroline worried that the trip would be too strenuous to be worthwhile. Putting the thought aside, she focused on copying William's papers, and conducting her sweeps.

'But you know we can see them more effectively from the ground, with our bare eyes,' Caroline argued, following William out towards the twenty-foot. 'You tried this last year, remember? I counted fifty in an hour; you saw only four.'

'One trial, Lina? Is that very good statistical material?' William grumbled. 'I thought you knew your mathematics better.'

Shaking her head, Caroline tried to bring his attention to the little platform she'd had the workmen set up earlier.

'Look, Brother – remember how the ground will sap our body heat right out of us? We'll be raised off the ground on these planks, and even have blankets. I made chocolate,' she said, pointing to the ornate samovar – a gift from Madamè D'Arblay – which burned merrily in the calm night, keeping the thick, dark liquid bubbling within.

'Bah, chocolate,' William muttered, climbing over the frame of the twenty-foot to adjust the height of the scope along the meridian.

It was late April, the peak of the Lyrid meteor shower. Generally known as 'shooting' or 'falling' stars, meteors were widely considered to be an atmospheric phenomenon, like lightning, rather than a cosmic one. But William's research pointed to something different. An astronomer in Italy named Giovanni Schiaparelli, who shared an interest in double stars, had worked out that the annual showers of falling stars coincided with the path of certain comets. Schiaparelli though that the meteor showers could actually be the *tails of comets*.

Caroline loved watching the meteor showers, especially with the idea that these flashes of light were the dusty tail blowing from a comet. It seemed like a grand version of the effect made by pulling a brand from the fire and waving it about in the dark: the body of the ember kept glowing, but sparks scattered into the darkness, shining for a brief moment before burning out.

The best way to watch a meteor shower was to lie flat, looking up into the heavens without the aid of the scope, thus viewing as much of the sky as possible. It became bone-achingly cold to lie directly on the grass, and this year Caroline had set everything up for a comfortable night of viewing, so they could count the Lyrids effectively, and enjoy doing so.

William seemed to want nothing to do with it. Something was wrong; he'd been curt for days, nagging at every little thing.

'Why won't this damn thing turn?' he snapped, fussing with a gear.

'William!' Caroline cried, unable to bear his foul mood any longer. 'Pray tell me the cause of your exasperation – it isn't the Lyrids, *or* the telescope.'

He paused, letting his hand drop from the gear, and sighed.

'I'm sorry, Lina,' he said quietly. 'Shall we have some chocolate? And I'll answer you.'

Handing him a wool rug to bundle into, for the air was cold and clear, Caroline wrapped herself in a rug, and served them both cups of steaming dark chocolate. It was a treat, and she would have to write to Fanny, thanking her for the samovar and blocks of drinking chocolate from France.

They settled onto the platform, side by side. Caroline waited.

Finally, William spoke.

'I proposed to Mary Pitt.'

It seemed the whole world had gone quiet. Caroline could not hear the horses in the stables, or doves in the hayloft, or even the wind in the trees. The statement had fallen from William heavily, and sat, heavily, before them.

'Proposed.' Caroline said. 'Marriage?'

William shot her an odd look. 'Yes, Sister, marriage.' He paused. 'However, I refused to give up either astronomy, or you as my assistant. And so Mary – Mrs Pitt – refused *me*.'

'*For you cannot have us both.*' Lalande's words rang in her ears.

But William evidently wanted…both. And now Mary had claimed the same as Lalande. '*Mary refused me.*'

'I did not realise,' Caroline said carefully, 'that you had such intimate feelings towards our neighbor.'

Wiliam drank down his chocolate, and then settled back on to the planks, his eyes up to the heavens. The Lyrids were beginning to fall, and she knew he was counting as each winked its brief luminescence across the sky.

'Yes,' he said. 'I do.'

She could not keep track of the meteors as they flickered through the night. While she had been entangled in her feelings for Lalande, William had been developing his own affection. From those first visits at Upton when John Pitt was unwell, to inviting Mary to dine at Obs House, Caroline should have seen it. She recalled the garden party, when Emmeline had staked her affection so highly on William. Even then, William's attention had been directed towards the Pitts. Even then, Caroline had been distracted by Lalande.

What she did not wish to dwell upon was the fact that William had not made the same decision as she: he had proposed to Mary, and the only reason he could not have them both was because of Mary's wishes, not his own.

It would have struck Caroline as the greatest betrayal of her life. As it had not come to pass, she chose to ignore it.

She reached over and patted her brother's hand.

'Forty-three,' he said quietly.

Since confessing the reason for his discontent, William's tension eased, but he remained unaware of how well Caroline understood his disappointment. She hated to see him unhappy, but she wanted his sacrifices to equal those she had made.

This was far from rational: William was a handsome, kind, successful man; there was no reason he should not wed if he wished. She had grown up thinking she would never have an offer of marriage, and this had proven true. If Lalande had proposed… but she could not think on it. The conclusion would have been the same. She was William's astronomical assistant, and she would remain as such, no matter what. The certainty of her role came from William as much as from herself, and she clung to it. He had refused to give up Caroline, and Mary had refused him.

As the month wore on, these thoughts sparked and collided within Caroline. William had become quiet, and she did not know what to expect. They carried on with their usual sweeps, and she assisted him as always, but she was waiting for him to say more.

'The Prince has gained the Regency,' William announced one morning over their breakfast of porridge and notes. 'Much will be changed when I – we – return to Court this spring.'

'You,' Caroline said, stirring nutmeg into her porridge. 'If it's not troublesome, I would rather not attend.'

William nodded. 'Perhaps, at a later time…' he trailed off. 'I'm sorry, Lina.'

Caroline looked at him quizzically, but he did not elaborate.

That afternoon, she could not find him in the workshop, in the house, or at the scopes.

She thought she would be sick with grief. Alexander's wife, with her weak constitution, was dead. The letter had arrived that afternoon. But it hardly bore on Caroline's mind at all.

She was sick with grief, for William had gone once again to Upton, to propose once again to Mary – and this time, she had accepted.

Burying her face in her ink-stained hands, Caroline sobbed. It was all too much. Alexander's world must be crashing around him, just as hers was.

'For you cannot have us both.'

But he would, curse it, William *would*. He could keep Caroline as his assistant. Mary had agreed to it, as long as Mary retained her home at Upton. Of course, this did not mean Mary would not move into Observatory House, oh no: the rich widow would keep *two* households. Would *run* two households. Caroline would lose all of her responsibility, all of her power, in the home she had managed for so long.

'But you shall still have the cottage, Lina,' William had said, oblivious to her dismay, 'and you shall have so much more time, which you can devote to astronomy – isn't it wonderful?'

She had fled. She'd run to the cottage and locked herself inside, where she wrote manically, pouring her bile into her journal. She cursed William for his affection towards Mary; cursed Mary for being pretty, and kind, and wealthy; even cursed John Pitt for dying. More than anything, she cursed herself for her blindness towards her brother. She had been living *his* life for so long, she no longer knew what she wanted; only made decisions based on what was best for them both – something William was clearly not inclined to do. She wrote until she exhausted the cruel words welling up within. She wrote the most unpleasant things she'd ever imagined, namely, about Mary Pitt, until she ran out of ink. The fading lines of words seemed to make her bitterness gradually fade, too.

She stopped, closing the journal, vowing never to read the horrible things inside.

She climbed from bed and peeked out the window. A clear night. Despite herself, it was not dancing, not needlework, not singing which pressed on her mind. Splashing her face with water from the basin, she dried off and tucked her hair into her bonnet. She pulled on an extra petticoat and wrapped a shawl around her shoulders before slowly climbing to the cottage roof where her reliable sweeper waited. She sat, and put her eye to the lens.

The stars were indifferent in their twinkling.

She might soon be usurped of minding William's household, but she could mind the heavens. Mary Pitt had no skill at *that*.

Chapter 20

On the green May morning when William wed Mary Pitt, Caroline sat in the front pew of the little church, back rod-straight, in a blue dress; a diminutive figure between Sir Joseph Banks and Dr William Watson. Mary's elderly mother and their neighbor Mrs Papendiek were also present, along with several acquaintances from Windsor.

Mary looked healthy in a white dress of sprig muslin, with a little white cap pinned to her brown hair. William, standing beside the altar, was dapper in a new jacket and trousers befitting his new title, for he was now Sir William Herschel, knighted recently at Windsor by the Regent. William was just over fifty-one years of age now; Mary, thirty-seven. They made a handsome couple. To anyone looking on, Mary was an ideal bride: she was wealthy but unpretentious, intelligent but not brilliant, sociable but not snobbish.

Indeed, Watson had admitted to encouraging William's interest in the young widow. He'd wanted his friend to lead a more normal life, he'd explained, not always caught up in the study of astronomy. Caroline had wanted to take Watson by the shoulders and shake him. What was the trouble, she wanted to ask, of being always caught up in astronomy?

On one hand, Caroline could admit that Watson's encouragement was well-intended. On the other, it was the cruelest thing her friend could have done, not to William, but to *her*. What of *her* chance to lead a normal life? She was thirty-eight, only a year older than Mary. Her father had been right: she was doomed to spinsterhood. At least she would keep her post as astronomical assistant. And she had her telescopes.

The voice of the elderly Vicar filled the church, and Caroline returned her attention to the ceremony.

'...continually bestow upon her your heart's deepest devotion, forsaking all others, keeping yourself only unto her as long as you both shall live?'

Caroline's shoulders stiffened. As her brother spoke his vows before her, she thought of one thing, other than a clear night, that she wanted. One thing which she could, with the Queen's annuity, afford to do.

William's voice was confident and clear. 'I do.'

She was moving out.

Dread. Dread perfectly described the state of mind in which Caroline found herself upon preparing to confront William. He would never understand her decision to leave Obs House – no, worse, once she *made* him understand, as she would have to, he would never forgive her. The choice flew in the face of his decision to wed. It was an insult to his new wife.

Going about her daily tasks, Caroline struggled to focus on the numbers in her calculations. Astronomy was precise work, and her mind, so used to steady, quiet focus, did not adapt easily to distractions. It took her twice as long as usual to finish a list of conversions for William, and when he asked for coffee after settling into his work late in the afternoon, she resolved to speak to him immediately. He was alone at the table, pouring over charts. Mary was at Upton, sorting out what would remain and what would be sent to her new home.

'Move out? But whatever for?' William asked, tugging his hands haphazardly through his greying hair. 'This is your home.'

'Home?' Caroline said. 'Home has been our house in Hanover; home has been New King Street in Bath; home has been Obs House in Slough. It will pain me to leave,

William, but it will pain me more to stay.' Caroline paused. 'Perhaps that is the meaning of home.'

'Now, Lina,' William pressed, not satisfied with her evasion. 'It's not Mary, is it? Come, Sister, I'm sure her presence at Obs House can only be pleasant to you – you've been the only woman, save Hannah, amidst all this work for a long time.'

For heaven's sake, Caroline thought, reaching into her pocket for her worry-bead, didn't he know she preferred it that way?

'Indeed, it may be rather a shock to Mary if you move out just as she intends to move in,' William said.

Caroline closed her eyes for a moment. Her brother was a brilliant man, she knew he was, but sometimes he was daft! She must tell him – God help her, he was too literal.

'Brother,' she said, pacing the carpet. 'I know it strikes you as odd, but please trust me. I've been considering it for some time now.' This was untrue; she'd only conceived of the idea at the wedding, but she went on. 'With my annuity, I can comfortably afford it.' This, at least, was true. She had done the calculations. 'I shall not move far, and I shall maintain my duties as your assistant, have no fear of that.'

'But Lina, I still don't understand why you wish to move out at all,' William said, gripping the back of the chair and looking at her in dismay. 'It's going to be damned inefficient.'

Caroline stopped pacing and looked him squarely in the eye. 'I cannot feel comfortable remaining under this roof when you now have –' she hesitated, and William raised a bushy eyebrow. '—a *wife*.' The word tasted bitter as it passed her lips.

William looked stunned.

'But, sister…' he stammered, 'I don't know what to say. Surely Mary's presence can only be a boon—'

'William,' Caroline broke in, 'I have run your household, from Bath to Windsor, since I was twenty-two years of age. I am now thirty-eight. Sixteen years! How can you think that introducing a –' again, she choked on the word, '— a *wife*, now, could be a pleasant occasion for me? How can I find endearing any woman whom I feel is only…replacing me?' The last words wavered in her throat.

William's face crumpled and he moved around the desk, reaching for her hand, but she pulled away, turning to stare into the fire.

'Oh Lina,' he said, 'You must *never* think I wish to replace you. You are my sister; my partner; my assistant. You are invaluable to me.'

Caroline grasped the worry-bead and nodded, still facing away.

'But what of love, Lina?' William continued, his voice soft. 'What of companionship? I have found these in Mary. Can you not be happy for us? For me?'

Caroline turned on him, tears flooding her eyes, blurring the lamplight. '*I too* found love, Brother. *I too* met with companionship. But I resisted – nay, *rejected* it, for our work. For *you*.'

She could control the anguish no longer, and tears began their cruel paths down her cheeks.

'But you did not make the same choice,' she whispered. 'You have betrayed me.'

Chapter 21

The wife of one of the workmen, the woman who, so long ago, fled at the sight of the wound in Caroline's thigh, had a spare room to let. Still ashamed at leaving Caroline in such distress, she'd offered a good price, and Caroline had accepted.

The room had low ceilings and a small hearth, but it was clean, with colourful woven rugs scattered upon the wooden floorboards. The single window peeped out onto a view of trees. There was a desk and chair, and a bed with a tick mattress was pushed against the whitewashed wall.

Caroline tidied away her few belongings, set her books on the desk, and left her dresses in the trunk. The low ceilings of the house did not encumber her; in fact, she felt the little room fit her perfectly.

She turned her confrontation with William over and over in her mind as she unpacked. If only she could stop seeing the sadness in her brother's eyes as she'd left. It wasn't as if she was returning to Hanover! She was only down the road, hardly twenty minutes' brisk walk to Obs House.

'*You have betrayed me*,' she'd said. The words rang true.

William had stared, unmoving, unfathomable. Finally, he spoke.

'I did not know, Lina.' His voice was tight. 'I did not know of the sacrifices you made. I did not know you disapproved of my choice.'

He made a strangled coughing sound, as if trying not to weep. Then he took a breath, and his voice was again even. 'But as you say, I have made it. I can only hope that

135

someday you will accept Mary, and love her as a sister.'
He paused.

The fire flickered in the hearth as the wind whistled down the chimney. Light shone in the depths of his troubled eyes.

'For now, all I can ask is that you remain cordial. All I can offer is my true wish for your happiness, and my regret that I have had any hand in preventing it.'

Caroline sat on the end of the bed in the unfamiliar room, and buried her face in her hands.

Her new orbit travelled from her rented room, to Observatory House, and back again, so Caroline fell into a pattern through the summer and into autumn. She copied her brother's papers, calculated and compiled his nebulae and double stars, and assisted him at the twenty-foot.

Meanwhile, Mary Herschel kept track of the household, mending her husband's clothing, serving his meals, and keeping him company in the evenings. Caroline would withdraw to her lodging, leaving them to share a book by the fireside or a song at the spinet. They always invited Caroline to join them; she always declined. The major difficulty was leaving her telescope behind: there simply was not a good place for her sweeper on the pitched roof of her new lodging, nor were the heavily-wooded grounds surrounding the house clear enough to see through. So Caroline often walked to and from Obs House twice a day, once for her daytime work, and again, after supper, for her work at the scopes. It was, as William had anticipated, inefficient, but she denied any inconvenience.

One task which William had been arranging as the nights became colder was the removal of the mirror from the twenty-foot. They would need a host of assistants to move the enormous disc, which needed repairing.

'Things will become frosty and slippery if we wait until too late in the year,' William explained, directing several men, including Watson, in loosening the fastenings.

Pulleys and tools lay scattered about the garden. Caroline stood high on the scaffold, balancing in the afternoon light, helping pass ropes that would secure the one-ton speculum before its move. She spotted Mary below, pacing. That woman needed a worry-bead of her own. Caroline wondered if Mary really had a fair concept of life at Observatory House upon accepting William's second proposal.

Mary looked up, shaking her head at the men and her sister-in-law clambering about the twenty-foot like ants on a woodpile.

It happened quickly. One moment, the ropes were secure; the next, the mirror was slipping – falling. Caroline shouted out, and everyone scattered. The scaffold rocked, Watson grabbed William, and there was a deafening crash, followed by a horrible silence.

Caroline scrambled down the scaffold so quickly she nearly fell, her petticoats snagging and tearing as she hastened to the ground.

Mary, sickly white, held William by the shoulders, looking him over from head to toe. For his part, William only looked startled.

'You are unharmed! Oh, my dear husband, thank heavens!' Mary cried, her brown eyes wild.

'Good God, man, that thing nearly crushed you!' Watson cursed.

Caroline's sharp eye counted the workmen. All were present. No one, then, was lying flattened beneath the mirror. She sucked in a breath of relief. The men, shaken, began to mill about, talking.

'Brother,' Caroline said, coming close, her throat still tight, 'were you nearest the speculum when it fell?' Her hands clasped open and shut, scraped raw from her rush to the ground, but the pain was nothing beside the relief coursing through her veins.

'Yes,' Mary answered for him. The colour was returning to her cheeks. Indeed, her face was becoming positively *red*. 'Yes, he was. Far too near! What were you thinking?'

William shook his head. 'I'm sorry…Yes. My wife is right. I shouldn't have been so close to the speculum. If it weren't for dear Watson…' he trailed off, blinked.

'My friend,' Watson said, grasping William by the shoulders. 'I have never told you this in all the time we've known each other, but –' he paused, stepping back. 'But I think you need a holiday.'

Caroline let out a small laugh. William, take a break? She'd never known him to go on holiday, ever. William gave his friend a look proving his thoughts matched those of his sister.

'Yes,' Mary chimed in, 'Dr Watson is right. We should travel. You should get away, my dear. Clear your head. Look at something *out* –the ocean, perhaps – rather than *up*.'

William's bushy eyebrows shot up in surprise, and Caroline watched in amazement.

Mary reached forward and took William's hand. 'A holiday, husband. For your own well-being – and for *mine*.'

There was a pause as they awaited William's reply. He would never acquiesce to the suggestion, even for Mary.

'You're right,' William said.

Watson and Mary let out matching sighs of relief. Caroline was dumbfounded.

'Yes,' William nodded. 'It is high time Mary and I go on holiday.' He smiled at his wife, squeezing her hand.

'Where shall we go, darling? It will be your choice entirely.'

So it was that late in the month of October, Caroline had Observatory House to herself. Upon reflection, she blessed Mary's sensible nature. Once, brother and sister would have pushed on from such an incident, perhaps with disastrous consequences. Once, she thought with a rueful chuckle, they'd both been fit for Bedlam.

Left alone to work in the house, with a fire burning in the hearth, Caroline took the journal in which she'd written her cruel thoughts about Mary, and consigned it to the flames.

Enjoying the chance to stay in her cottage rooms again, Caroline bustled about on the flat roof, inspecting her reflecting telescope and readying for nightfall. She'd missed the sweeper dreadfully since moving out, but was pleased to see it in fine condition. The mahogany angles, the cool smell of wood, the crisp magnification through the lens: this wonderful instrument enabled her to discover nebulae and comets to her heart's content.

When night fell, the stars leapt from the sky, familiar as old friends. She noted her coordinates, the date and time, oriented her position along the meridian, and began to sweep. She rubbed her hands together to force out the chill. The air was just cold enough to think of wearing her woolen gloves, her extra petticoats, and her shawls, but she remembered those were not packed right downstairs in her cottage, but twenty minutes' walk away, in her rented room. She stomped her feet and tried to ignore the cold.

It was pleasant to be back at Observatory House, sweeping, but it felt odd to be alone there. When William had been to the Continent, or at Windsor, she'd enjoyed the independence, the solitude. Perhaps it was because she knew Lalande would not be walking up the drive to meet her, or perhaps it was Mary's ownership over the household, leaving a gap even with her absence. Despite the shift and collision of their lives, she had always been kind towards Caroline. Whatever the reason, Caroline found herself missing the flicker of a lamp down in the parlour, the shout of William's instructions at the twenty-foot. She even rather missed Mary venturing outdoors to offer coffee. And she unquestionably missed her breakfasts at Obs House: sitting silently with her porridge by the hearth was dismal compared to her discussions with William. She hated the thought that he might engage Mary with such ideas, rather than her.

A small, faint blur caught her attention, and she focused beside it, the familiar tingle of discovery creeping into her fingertips. It was bound to be a comet. After noting its coordinates and drawing a sketch, she traced its path through the sky for nearly an hour. She smiled. She would write to Maskelyne immediately, but first, she must tell William –

She turned, blinking, from the scope, and stopped. But William was away – on holiday, with his wife.

Frowning, she made her way not to the house, but to the stables, where she sought out Erik. Gently shaking him awake, she instructed the bleary-eyed lad to ready William's old mare, and then she withdrew to the house to prepare a satchel, stuffing her notes from the night's sweeps into a leather bag along with bread, cheese, and one of Mary's shawls. She threw on her cloak and returned to the stables, where Erik had made sure all was ready.

'Miss, are you certain…' he asked, puzzled to see her riding at all, and so late at night.

'Thank you, Erik,' she said, tousling his hair. 'I'll be fine.'

She hoped she was right as she urged the horse into a trot, making her way down the dark path. Once away from the house, they broke into a gallop. Dirt flew beneath the horse's hooves as they went. The road was wide, and they seemed to be the only creatures awake for miles around.

The hour was late, the air was cold, but Caroline did not care a fig. She galloped past tall trees and darkened houses, her hair tangling in the wind. She relished the exhilaration of speed, the clean whisper of frost on her tongue. Her ears grew numb, and all was silent save the hoof-beats matching her pounding heart. A woman travelling alone at night, when no one knew her whereabouts. Was she mad?

She laughed aloud. Probably.

Allowing the mare to slow to a canter, Caroline arched her head towards the night sky, in the direction of her latest comet. It was not visible without the aid of a telescope, but she knew it was there, and soon others would, too, for she would deliver the news herself.

She was finally going to Greenwich.

Chapter 22

On her guard, Caroline picked her way through the sleeping streets of London in the early dawn. She had read enough letters from William's travels to and from the city to know to take the main road to Richmond, and then follow the river to Greenwich.

Sleeping, rag-wrapped bundles huddled in doorways. Rats made furtive journeys to and from filth-laden gutters. But little else stirred, and Caroline was grateful. The mare had grown tired, and it would be difficult to make her gallop should there be trouble. The wind was down, and the stench of the city rose up from its weft and weave of alleyways, reeking of every sort of waste. Caroline endeavoured to keep her breaths short, and her eyes sharp.

London unnerved her. Usually because of the bustle, the noise, the crowds. She had never seen it asleep. As she rode along the south bank of the Thames, she didn't dare look down, for fear of identifying the dark shapes bobbing in the river's dark waters. The mare's hooves clopped loudly on cobblestones as they passed the narrow entrance to London Bridge; the noise hastened as the horse made for a watering trough. Caroline chewed a seed bun as the mare drank. She vaguely recalled William's mention of a competition for a new bridge design; the present one was over six hundred years old and falling apart. She was relieved she needn't cross it. A breeze danced off the river, causing a sign to creak above her, and she looked up. Why, she had been here before!

The image painted on the sign – a pair of spectacles – took her back years. Her first impression of London was that it had been full of nothing but optical shops. William had wanted to stop nowhere else. At the time, exhausted from their journey, Caroline could only trail behind William like a wraith. She recalled blearily wondering why her brother was interested in optical lenses when he had perfectly good eyesight. Then they'd proceeded to Bath, and she'd been swept up in life at the Octagon and New King Street. It was only later that she'd made the connection: lenses, telescopes. From her first days in England, William's obsession had been evident. She'd simply failed to see it.

Caroline urged the mare along. The city was beginning to stir, and she did not wish to be caught in the morning fray of fishmongers, chimney sweeps, washwomen and pickpockets.

Caroline passed docks and shipyards. She passed gently swaying sailboats; she passed the looming hulks of hospital ships. Finally, she reached a row of great trees. Pausing, she listened, and made out the soft, whispering thud of chestnuts as they freed themselves from the trees high above and fell to the ground. The mare shied.

'Hush, now,' Caroline soothed, 'We've nearly arrived.'

High on the lush autumnal hill, past a flock of grazing sheep, stood the Royal Observatory with its towers, gleaming windows, and two domes housing telescopes. Flamsteed House, the main building and face of the Observatory, cast a benevolent eye upon the park and down to the Thames. William had described it to her, this fairy-castle of red brick and white trim. The main room in Flamsteed House was called the Octagon Room, a space created for observing celestial activity: transits, eclipses, even comets. From one Octagon to another, Caroline thought with tired relief.

In fact, William had explained, when the house was built in 1675, it had been erected on the wrong spot. To make observations from the true Meridian line, Astronomers Royal since Flamsteed's day had to work from a shed on the grounds of the Observatory, all the while keeping it a secret from their patron, King Charles. Caroline quietly chuckled– it was so charming, so bumbling. So *English*.

Despite the missteps, the Observatory had been founded by King Charles II to help sailors navigate at sea – too many merchant ships, too many expensive goods, and too many precious lives had been lost in uncharted waters. A reliable map of the heavens, suitable for navigation upon the otherwise featureless ocean, was needed, and Flamsteed was the man to do it. Caroline tried not to think about how many errors she'd corrected in his Star Catalogue; it had been a good effort, a vast improvement from the dearth of information before. She was grateful for the opportunity to further improve it.

Looking up the steep hill, to the very top of the building, Caroline's eye traced a path to a mast, on which a red ball sat. That must be the Time Ball: raised at 12:58 and lowered at 13:00 precisely, every day, the signal allowed ships moored on the Thames to set their own time-pieces accordingly. Greenwich was the centre of time as it related to England, and the sea. A different sort of astronomy, in the main, from the work she and William carried out. But she, her brother, and Dr Maskelyne shared an understanding of the skies, and now, finally, she could accept the Astronomer Royal's invitation.

The door was answered by a sleepy assistant who showed Caroline into the parlour. She sank into an upholstered chair, rubbing cramps from her aching muscles, while the boy went to announce her. He returned with news that the Maskelynes would soon be breakfasting, and wished her to join them.

*

'And so you rode here all on your own?' Sophia gasped. 'Your fortitude amazes me!'

Despite a translucence of skin which hinted at a lack of sunlight, Sophia Maskelyne was animated by Caroline's story. If the couple were startled by Caroline's solo appearance, they were too polite to betray it, but Caroline reckoned they were used to a stream of more or less eccentric visitors, just as she and William were.

Indeed, it was the Herschel siblings' very reputation for eccentricity, as well as the favour of the King, which allowed Caroline to do things other ladies could not, from greeting strangers late at night for tours of the telescopes, to balancing atop the twenty-foot to help dismantle it. If she had been young, or rich, or eligible, such activities might have tarnished her character, but she was well beyond heeding convention, and relished her freedom.

'I have so dearly wished to meet you,' Sophia repeated, pressing Caroline's hand. 'Too few women understand what it is like to be wholly devoted to a man who himself is wholly devoted to the study of astronomy.' She smiled at her husband, who waggled his white eyebrows knowingly as he turned pieces of toast over the fire for their breakfast.

'Do you recall our first meeting?' Dr Maskelyne asked with a chuckle, and Caroline smiled.

'Oh, I was horrified to have asked if you *knew of Messier*,' she cried, 'I hadn't the foggiest idea whom I was speaking to!'

Maskelyne nodded, distributing the toast, and offered a tray of jams. 'Ah, but even then, you knew the facts of what you described,' he said, 'and I was most impressed; most impressed. You called it your brother's *hobby*, do you recall?'

'Oh yes,' Caroline said. 'Little did I know that he would play Copernicus, swapping music for astronomy as that man swapped the earth for the sun.'

'And at the centre of *your* universe?' Sophia asked. She unlocked the tea chest, and Caroline was relieved to see her take out coffee.

'Do all astronomers rely on coffee through their waking hours?' Caroline asked.

'Our waking hours should be that much shorter without it,' Maskelyne said, pushing the kettle over the fire.

There was a pause while Caroline considered Sophia's question.

'Well, Mrs Maskelyne, I came to Greenwich to visit you both, of course,' Caroline said, 'but also to say I've found another comet.' The tingling returned to her fingertips.

'Extraordinary!' Maskelyne said, smacking his knee in delight.

Sophia clasped her hands and smiled. 'How many is that now, Miss Herschel?'

'Eight,' Caroline said.

'You must point out your comet as soon as it's dark enough,' Maskelyne said. 'It may well be another strike against Messier, and cause for us to celebrate.'

After breakfast, Sophia showed Caroline to a guest bedroom.

'Don't worry, Miss Herschel,' she said, 'I understand the need to sleep in the day, and work through the night. If I did not adjust my own rhythm of sleep, I would never see my husband.'

The cackling of a crow woke Caroline from deep sleep. It took a moment to recall where she was, and when she did, she smiled. She'd done it. She'd ridden to Greenwich on her own, and reported her eighth comet to the Astronomer Royal.

The crow chattered a second time, and she forced herself to rise. Deciding to stop in the parlour first to seek her hosts, Caroline paused on the stairwell to peer through a window overlooking the park. Sunset threw long shadows over the green hill, and hundreds of chestnuts glowed in the grass, a burnished scattering of fallen meteors.

'The chestnuts are delicious roasted,' Sophia said, appearing at the top of the stair with a lantern. 'Though take care they don't fall upon your head – they smart!'

The crow let out a particularly loud squawk, and Caroline laughed. 'My, that's a chatty bird! It woke me.'

Sophia shook her head, passing Caroline on the stair and gesturing for her to follow. 'I do apologise. It roosts just above that window, and makes a racket whenever we have guests. This way, please.'

Caroline followed her hostess along a corridor, past the empty parlour.

'Despite the disruption, we consider that bird good luck,' Sophia explained as Caroline followed her thin, lamp-lit outline down the hall. 'There are many myths surrounding the Observatory, you see. Have you heard of the ravens before?'

'I'm afraid I haven't, Mrs Maskelyne,' Caroline admitted, curious. Their skirts rustled along the polished wood of the empty hall.

'The first Astronomer Royal, John Flamsteed, worked from the Tower of London whilst the Observatory was under construction,' Sophia explained. 'But the ravens would often perch upon – and of course, foul up, ahem,' she cleared her throat, 'the telescopes.'

'A nuisance indeed,' Caroline said. There was no greater frustration, save perhaps an insect crawling across the lens, startling her out of her wits. Any leggy, winged creature unsuspectingly landing on the wrong part of the scope could appear as a monster to the viewer.

'Well,' Sophia continued, 'King Charles was apparently on the verge of shooting the ravens – or at least ordering them dispatched – when someone told him of the prophecy: when the ravens leave the Tower, the Tower and he who rules it will fall. Thus, Charles spared the pesky birds, and Flamsteed had to contend with the mess until he moved to Greenwich.'

'And so this crow is a bird of luck, visiting, as it were, from the Tower.' Caroline finished.

'A bird of luck, and a lucky bird,' Sophia said, stopping. They'd reached a spiral staircase leading to one of the two domes. 'I'm amazed at how superstitious men seeking the 'Truth of Nature' can be. Here we are. My husband will be upstairs, working.' She gestured for Caroline to ascend, and followed after.

The dome was opened to the darkening sky, and Maskelyne stood with a pair of assistants, deep in conversation, leaning over a paper-strewn table. The scene was familiar, though rather than double stars, Maskelyne was discussing the *Nautical Almanac*. Upon their approach, he dismissed the assistants and asked Caroline for the coordinates of her comet.

'…And there it is,' Maskelyne said, peering through a familiar telescope. It had been made, of course, by William, commissioned for Greenwich, and thus Caroline knew it was accurate.

'I have written, *'Messier has it not'*,' she said, pointing to her notes. 'It appears in none of his charts.'

Maskelyne strode to the table and rifled through his papers, moving a lantern close so he could better see. He pulled out a well-thumbed volume, flipped through it, and read. After a moment, he nodded.

'Right again, Miss Herschel,' he said.

Sophia gave a little clap of her hands. 'Miss Herschel's eighth comet,' she said. 'This is indeed an achievement! What an honour to have you here.'

'Thank you,' Caroline said, gratitude blooming warm throughout her. 'It is so much pleasanter to celebrate this in person,' she continued, gesturing to her hosts, 'rather than through a letter. It does my heart good.'

'It is truly wonderful,' Sophia murmured.

Dr Maskelyne shuttered the lantern and gestured to the sky. 'Just think, Miss Herschel,' he said, his voice clear in the dark, 'There are more stars in the universe than there have been heartbeats in the entirety of human existence. We may not know exactly how vast it is, but even the ancient Greeks were able to extrapolate ideas of the cosmos that we still use today. Just like the seafarers I attempt to aid in navigating the oceans, you and your brother strike out into the unknown every night. You have learnt to navigate the skies. You are helping us all to find our way through this sea of questions – questions of existence, and time.'

'You might say you are helping us to find our way home, Miss Herschel,' Sophia added quietly, 'in a cosmological sense.'

Caroline smiled. Such talk was reminiscent of that which she so missed at the breakfast table with William. Tilting her head, she drank in the ocean of starlit sky. Indeed, many landmarks – constellations, asterisms, meteor showers and double stars – had become familiar. And there was still much to discover.

She knew what she must do. After her visit to Greenwich, she would ride back to Observatory House, and once William and Mary returned, she would ask to move back to the cottage. She belonged there, sweeping the skies from her rooftop, and working at William's side.

She would tell them of her eighth comet, and she would ask to come home.

Chapter 23

1816

The Queen was hosting a fête at her favourite country estate, Frogmore House, for her seventy-second birthday. Ensconced in his routine at Obs House, and almost eighty years of age, William expressed no desire to make the journey.

It was a hot afternoon in July, and Caroline walked slowly with William around the lawns. At times, he was unsteady on his feet, and she was careful not to hurry him. The Queen's birthday was in May, but she'd decided to host the fête later in the summer, when the nights were longer. Caroline and William discussed the invitation as they pottered about, collecting raspberries in a basket.

'They Royal couple have done so much for us, William. I'm sorry you don't wish to go,' Caroline said.

William smiled. 'The tables have turned, Sister. I was always running off to Windsor, and now, I don't feel inclined to run anywhere. You must go; take John with you.'

Caroline nodded, thinking of the dress and jewellery she would need to unearth in order to be presentable. John would enjoy the visit, though – her beloved nephew was already twenty-four, down from Cambridge for the summer. How swiftly time passed.

William considered a raspberry before popping it into his mouth. 'Each its own little universe,' he mused, holding it between gnarled fingers. Caroline smiled. Her brother was growing sentimental in his old age. She recalled when those fingers were long and elegant, drawing out tunes from the oboe or violoncello. She recalled when they were rough and calloused, grinding lenses and blending pitch. She recalled when they were ink-stained and smudged, scrawling out brilliant philosophical papers. Now they were crabbed, berry streaked, and quivered with a slight tremor. His white hair was so thin it was nearly gone, floating in wisps about the crown of his head. Though still tall, his posture was hunched, undoubtedly from all that time at the scopes.

'Time is strange, isn't it, Lina?' William asked, the wrinkles on his brow furrowing. 'Its path is unfathomable, yet there I was, trying to chart it all.' The skin around his eyes melted into a lacework of creases as he smiled at her. 'And you were there, for everything.' He offered her a handful of berries.

As with anything, she absently counted. Eight. She rolled them in the palm of her hand, where they collided gently, leaving trails of juice along her weathered skin. The sun warmed their shoulders and hands. For all their counting, they couldn't hold on to the metronomic passing of the seasons, marked by the long-case clock in the dining room, which, when wound down, brought heartbeats to mind.

John handed Caroline up into the carriage, sent by Princess Augusta to collect them. The clever girl had expressed an interest in mathematics, and had visited Caroline at Obs House once or twice in the past, recalling with pleasure the famous garden party so many summers ago. The carriage was a kind thought, a small gesture of continued patronage.

'I'm pleased you're joining me. You always were my shadow, little nephew,' Caroline said, patting John's hand as he settled into the facing seat. He smiled, and his brown eyes reminded her of his father's.

'It was because you were small, like me,' he said.

151

'And now you're taller than your father,' Caroline sighed. 'I mustn't call you *little* nephew anymore.'

They set off at a slow pace, and the spars of the forty-foot peeked out from behind the roof of Obs House. John had loved clambering up and down the scaffolding when he was younger, frustrating his father and frightening his mother.

'He's always climbing places he shouldn't, getting into things he mustn't,' William had complained.

Caroline had laughed. 'Yes – just as you used to, Brother.'

'You so enjoyed scaling the rigging, didn't you, John?' Caroline said, following her nephew's gaze to the telescope, which shrank in the distance as the carriage rolled on.

John nodded. 'A shame the old thing is rotting away,' he said, 'but we make a good team at the twenty-foot, don't we, Aunt Lina?'

'Indeed we do, my boy,' she answered, thinking of how natural the handover had been from father to son, how easy it had been for John to step into William's place as William had become less able to stand out in the cold.

'Indeed, we do.'

At Frogmore House, in the yellow-panelled Library, Caroline was approached by a graceful, grey-haired woman.

'Miss Herschel,' Emmeline said, grasping her friend's hands. 'You've hardly aged a day, my dear.'

'Let us say we're all changed, but gracefully so,' Caroline said, knowing that her own hair, faded white, and the wrinkles around her eyes, betrayed the effects of time just as honestly as they did upon her friend. 'Have you news of Madame D'Arblay, Emmeline? I do wish we three could be together again, to share a glass of wine, and laugh over our heartaches and triumphs.'

'Ah, our dear Fanny,' Emmeline said, her look growing serious. 'Have you not heard? The poor darling had to undergo the most barbaric of surgeries – she survived, mind,' she hastened to add, 'but God, to think of her bravery in the face of such a thing.'

'Great heavens, what happened?' Caroline asked, leaning close. Her friend had been kind and generous; she hated the idea of her suffering.

Emmeline's voice dropped to a whisper. 'Cancer,' she said, 'of the breast. The operation was a success; she is convalescing in France. They held her down and cut right into her. Not a whit of decency, I'm sure.' She shook her head, gestured to a servant, and plucked two glasses of port from his silver tray.

'Brave indeed,' Caroline murmured, accepting the drink. Dressing her own wound that New Year's Eve had taken every bit of her strength, and still she'd fainted dead away. She couldn't imagine what her friend's pain had been, under a surgeon's knife. Dear Fanny! At least the lady would use *that* tale in a book. People would read of the episode far and wide, no doubt.

'Gracious,' Caroline said as a gilded clock high on the wall chimed the hour. Little doors snapped open and a troupe of wooden courtiers twirled out, along a little path, and back into the clock. The doors snapped shut. The day had slipped away from her.

'Do pardon me, my friend,' she said, giving Emmeline a kiss on the cheek. 'I must find my nephew. We don't wish to be late returning home – we promised to tell William all the news we heard today.'

Caroline made her way past sunset-flooded windows, searching for John, and ended up outside on a terrace. Not far in the distance, the familiar bulk of Windsor

Castle glowed with a warm sandy shade, reminiscent of summer days in Bath, when the city stretched languid and handsome under a rare, cloudless sky.

'*Mais non*, Sir, you will fall. *Viens ici*!'

A high, concerned voice drew Caroline's attention. Curious, she followed the commotion around a corner. A young woman in an elegant gown, with dark curls flowing down her back, stood looking up at a chimney-stack. Her stance, hands on hips, eyes flashing, contrasted with the sweetness of her voice. Caroline followed the young woman's gaze, and sighed. John clung near the top of the chimney, looking out over the gardens.

'It's quite safe, I say,' he replied to the girl. He had yet to notice his aunt. 'And the views are excellent! Shall I help you up?'

'*Non*,' the girl growled. Caroline admired the temper in her voice. '*You will fall.*'

Caroline stepped forward, about to intervene, when a voice called her name.

'*Carolina*!'

The girl spun around. '*Alors*, Papa! *Je suis ici*!'

Footsteps sounded on the terrace, and Caroline turned, too. Now she was the one falling. Lalande.

He slowed, recognition dawning on his face. He'd weathered well, his wrinkles giving him an elegant air. His head was smooth and bald as ever, his eyes as blue. He approached, his black-gloved hand tightening atop a walking stick.

The sun had almost closed its eye on the horizon, and Caroline was grateful for the forgiving evening light. She heard John's quiet footfall as he climbed to the terrace.

An age passed before anyone spoke.

'Aunt Lina?' John murmured, taking a hesitant step in her direction.

'Forgive me,' Caroline said, and Lalande followed in almost the same breath, '*Non, mademoiselle*, forgive *me* –'

The girl took the cue to make an elegant curtsey.

'So this…?' Caroline asked, her voice faltering.

'Carolina,' Lalande said, with a tilt of his head. 'My daughter.' He turned to the girl. 'Darling, this is the brilliant lady after whom you are named.'

The girl's eyes widened, and she curtseyed again. '*Enchanté*,' she murmured. 'You are the famous lady *astro-no-mer*, who finds comets?'

John grinned, nodding. 'Yes: my Aunt. The best Lady Astronomer in the world.'

'Hush, dear,' Caroline said, a smile playing on her lips, sparring with the tears that threatened to prick her eyes.

In the distance, the bells of Windsor Castle's chapel began to chime.

'Papa! Mama will wonder where we are,' the girl said, touching her father's arm.

'Yes, darling, we shall go,' Lalande whispered.

Caroline's eyes met her old love's pale, pale blue ones. There was the familiar intelligence; there, the familiar kindness. Along with which, Caroline espied another universe: one she had sacrificed altogether.

155

New Year's Day, 1840

My Dear Aunt,

We hope you are well in Hanover. Please send our love to Dietrich and his family. I know you don't much care for gifts, but do tell me something special we can send for your 90th birthday – it would greatly please me, Maggie, and the children.

How I wish you could have joined us last night! I was finally able to re-create those wonderful tales you used to regale me with of Garden Parties and concerts held in the tube of the great forty-foot telescope.

As you know, the forty-foot was falling apart in the wind, and last year's storm finally crushed the monstrous contraption beneath a tree branch. The rigging has been rotting and dangerously loose for years – you know best how precarious the thing was, even when newly built. Thus I hope you are pleased to hear that Father's great telescope, which has been a corridor to the stars for Kings and Bishops, novelists and explorers, was given due ceremony in its final moments.

You see, Aunt Lina, I wrote a song. You always told me how twined Father's music and astronomy were, so, as we drank the health of our young Queen Victoria, we put the great tube to rest with music and cheers; a 'happy dirge,' if you will.

I like to think Father was smiling down on us for the occasion, from somewhere beyond his double stars. All is at rest now. I enclose the song for your enjoyment.

Ever your affectionate nephew,

J.F.W. Herschel

Hymn of the Forty Feet Reflector at Slough,
Sung on New Year's Eve, 1839-40, by the whole
family in the Tube thereof assembled:

In the old Telescope's tube we sit,
And the shades of the past around us flit;
His requiem sing we with shout and with din,
While the old year goes out and the new comes in.

Merrily, merrily, let us all sing,
And make the old Telescope rattle and ring.

Full fifty years did he laugh at the storm,
And the blast could not shake his majestic form;
Now prone he lies where he once stood high,
And searched the deep heaven with his broad bright eye.

Merrily, merrily, let us all sing,
And make the old Telescope rattle and ring.

He hath stretched him quietly down at length
To bask in the starlight his giant strength;
And time shall here a tough morsel find,
For his steel-devouring teeth to grind.

Merrily, merrily, let us all sing,
And make the old Telescope rattle and ring.

He will grind it at last, as grind it he must,
And its brass and its iron shall be clay and dust;
But scathless ages shall roll away,
And nurture its frame in its form's decay.

Merrily, merrily, let us all sing,
And make the old Telescope rattle and ring.

There are wonders no living wight hath seen,
Which within this hollow have pictured been,
Which mortal record can ne'er recall,
And are known to Him only who made them all.

Merrily, merrily, let us all sing,
And make the old Telescope rattle and ring!

Afterword

The Royal annuity of £50, granted by the Queen in 1787, made Caroline the first woman in England to earn a salary from scientific work. She discovered eight comets in her lifetime, corrected Flamsteed's Star Catalogue, and assisted William invaluably.

After William died in 1822 at eighty-four years of age, Caroline returned to Hanover. There, she was treated as a celebrity. She maintained copious correspondence with her family in England.

Back in the town where she held bitter memories of her youth, Caroline often found fault with her youngest brother Dietrich and his family, with whom she lived. She remained in Hanover, though her letters express endless lament over leaving England.

In 1835, she and Mary Somerville were the first women to be elected to Honorary Membership of the Royal Astronomical Society. In 1838 Caroline was elected to membership of the Royal Irish Academy, and in 1846 the King of Prussia awarded her the Gold Medal for Science.

Caroline fiercely wished she were young and spry enough to accompany her nephew, John, whom she adored only slightly less than his father, on his voyage to the Cape, where he carried on his father's work of charting double stars in the Southern hemisphere – stars William and Caroline would never have seen.

In Hanover, Caroline frequented the theatre and had a reputation for sprightliness even in her later years. She died twenty-six years after William, at the age of ninety-eight.

Acknowledgements

The first time I heard of Caroline Herschel was through a 20-minute biography of her life told by Simon Nosworthy at the Royal Observatory, Greenwich. Simon's admiration of Caroline's endurance and adaptability made me want to know more.

The staff at the ROG proved most encouraging, and I want to especially thank Marek Kukula for access to archives, as well as enthusiasm about the project. It was a great delight to work on the book within one of the Observatory's domes.

I am deeply indebted to the Herschel-Shorland family, especially John Herschel-Shorland and his daughter, Cassie Herschel-Shorland, for their assistance, encouragement, and friendship. They welcomed me into their homes, allowing me to examine letters, pictures and ephemera, from Caroline's remaining dress, to the long-case clock. Our trip to Bath for the Herschel AGM was a special treat.

Through her MA in Archaeological Illustration, Cassie reconstructed an historically credible image of Caroline in her 20s (no images of her at this age existed to this point,) and I'm especially honoured that, using her research from the MA, Cassie designed the book cover for *Double the Stars*.

I want to thank my friends and family for their continuous support in my writing. These projects would not come to fruition without such encouragement. Special thanks go to Richard Barnett and Caitlin Wylie for patiently editing numerous versions of this text.

A role as poet-in-residence at the Whipple Museum of the History of Science, University of Cambridge, from 2009 – 2012, allowed time to work on drafts whilst considering one of William's remaining telescopes. I am grateful to the Museum for their support during the residency – especially to Liba, Claire, and Steve – and would like to particularly thank Dr Melanie Keene for bringing my attention to the 'Hymn of the Forty Feet Reflector at Slough,' a real song performed as described.

A grant from The Authors' Foundation in 2009 provided time towards early drafts of the book, and I am grateful for that support.

Heartfelt thanks to my editor Jan at Cinnamon Press, who has guided the book into its final draft, and has given me the encouragement needed to complete the project.

Further Resources

- The primary resource for researching Caroline's story is a compilation of her memoirs, *Memoir and Correspondence of Caroline Herschel,* assembled with commentary by Mrs. John Herschel and first published by John Murray in 1876; second ed. 1879.

- A close second is *The Herschel Chronicle: The Life-Story of William Herschel and his Sister Caroline Herschel,* edited by his Granddaughter Constance A. Lubbock, printed by Cambridge University Press, 1933.

- For a version of William's story with some mention of Caroline, not told by members of the family, I highly recommend *The Age of Wonder: How the Romantic Generation Discovered the Beauty and Terror of Science,* by Richard Holmes, published by Harper Press, 2009.

- A brief non-fiction piece on Caroline, *The Comet Sweeper: Caroline Herschel's Astronomical Ambition,* by Claire Brock, published by Icon Books in 2007, is a pleasant introduction to Caroline's work.

- Historian Michael Hoskin is the foremost academic on the Herschels, and his publications are numerous and thorough: www.michaelhoskin.com

- The Herschel Museum of Astronomy is an excellent place to visit to learn more about the siblings' life in Bath. The Science Museum and Royal Observatory Greenwich in London, the Oxford Museum of the History of Science, and The Whipple Museum of the History of Science in Cambridge, all hold Herschel ephemera, and are all worthy of many visits.

Kelley Swain was born in Rhode Island and lives in London. She is the author of *Atlantic* (Cinnamon Press, 2014), *Opera di Cera* (Valley Press, 2014), *Darwin's Microscope* (Flambard Press, 2009), and editor of *Pocket Horizon* (Valley Press, 2013), and *The Rules of Form: Sonnets and Slide Rules* (Whipple Museum, 2012). From 2009 – 2012, Kelley was poet-in-residence at the Whipple Museum of the History of Science in Cambridge. She is a member of the Greenwich-based Nevada Street Poets and a Fellow of the Linnean Society of London.